A WHISPER IN THE BAY

CHASING TIDES BOOK ONE

FIONA BAKER

Published in the United States of America

First Edition, 2022

fionabakerauthor.com

JOIN MY NEWSLETTER

If you love beachy, feel-good women's fiction, sign up to receive my newsletter, where you'll get free books, exclusive bonus content, and info on my new releases and sales!

CHAPTER ONE

Alissa Lewis rested her elbows on her desk and massaged her temples, wishing the motion would dislodge the words she was looking for from her brain. It wasn't working. The page on her screen was just as bare as before—just a single sentence that she needed to rewrite. At least it got to the point of what her article was supposed to be about.

Well, maybe. The article was supposed to be about a craft kombucha company that was growing in the Denver area, but the one sentence she had written made it sound so... blah. But when she talked to the company's co-owners, their enthusiasm and passion was so interesting. It just wasn't coming across on the page and she wasn't sure of what to do.

Alissa heaved a sigh, earning her a glance from

her coworker across the open floor plan. She shrugged in response and turned her attention back to the screen. Getting this job at *Epic News* had been Alissa's dream ever since she picked up her first newspaper in high school. It was filled with engaging stories and in-depth articles on subjects that other papers didn't always even cover, all put together in a surprisingly cool-looking package.

She had imagined the writers there living glamorous lives, typing away and finding out about burgeoning industries that Denver had to offer before everyone else.

That definitely wasn't her reality—her workdays usually involved staring at a blank screen and trying to scrape words out of the depths of her brain as deadlines loomed over her head. She didn't have the fun, challenging conversations with her coworkers that she'd hoped for, just petty rivalries and awkward talk about the coffee in the break room. In fact, she couldn't remember the last time that she talked to one of her coworkers beyond a hello. The most they interacted was through the sighs across the open floor plan.

On top of that, the big break she'd been hoping for was more of a small jump into the pond. But this was the newspaper industry. It took time to climb up the ladder to where she wanted to be and she had to stick it out.

Alissa pushed forward on her article, just trying to put words down. It was easier to edit something rather than nothing. That helped her in the rare moments when she wrote something for fun these days, but here it wasn't helping that much. It was too late for a cup of coffee, so she tried to outline her work in the document, jotting down bullet points of the ideas she needed to include. That helped, at least a little.

But right when she got into a groove, she had to go to a meeting, and after that, a call with someone she planned to interview took up another hour of her time. By the end of the day, her brain felt dried up and she had gone from one sentence to several paragraphs, three of which she knew she'd have to delete later. That was a problem for future Alissa.

She saved her document twice for good measure, then put on her down jacket and gathered her things in her canvas tote bag. Even though this article wasn't working out, she hoped the last one she had turned in, a story on a music industry conference, had impressed her boss, Stanley Rush. He was half the reason why she wanted to work at *Epic*. His articles were the most engrossing of all the staff writers by far. Every time Alissa wrote an article, she wanted to impress him. But that was a goal she rarely hit on the first try.

The article had been a struggle, much like the one she had worked on most of the day. Stanley hadn't given her his feedback on it yet, but she felt it had come out okay. She'd gotten some great quotes from attendees that gave the article flavor. That was one of her favorite parts of the job—talking to people and getting their stories. Unfortunately, talking to people about their work or their companies often got her canned answers that had to be approved by some higher-ups before they got published.

On rare occasions, she got more earnest responses. Those always made her work so much easier, at least most of the time. Being able to tap into someone's excitement about what they loved to do always spurred her on. She just wished that she could figure out how to take the kombucha guys' passion and put it into words.

She shook off thoughts of work, especially since it was Friday. All she wanted to do was get home and eat a big, warm bowl of soup in front of the TV. It wasn't the most exciting evening, but it was just what she needed. She was a relatively solitary person in general, mostly spending nights in. She couldn't even remember the last time she'd gone on a date, not that she was necessarily looking for love.

"Alissa," Stanley said as she passed by his office on her way out. "Can I talk to you for a moment?"

Her stomach dropped when she saw the seriousness of his expression. "Sure, of course."

She stepped inside of his office. Unlike her glorified cubicle, Stanley's office had a million dollar view of Denver. Even the heavy clouds and snow that everyone expected in early January didn't take away from its beauty—the lights of the city shined through the darkness, creating an almost cozy feeling in the modern style of the office's decor.

Alissa gently closed the door behind her and sat in one of the stylish, uncomfortable chairs in front of Stanley's desk. She resisted the urge to push her curls out of her face, wedging her folded hands between her thighs. Even though she had worked for Stanley for a few years, she still found him slightly intimidating. He was tall and imposing, with an angular face that made him look stern even when he was in a good mood. Plus, he was incredible at what he did. Scrutinizing her work with his skilled eye always cranked up her nerves.

"I wanted to talk to you about your last two articles—the one that was published and the one you just turned in." Stanley folded his hands together and rested them on his desk. "The one that was published in our previous issue wasn't well-received."

A knot tightened in Alissa's chest. "Oh. Um, what did people say about it?"

"It was more of what they didn't say," he said. "The engagement for the online piece was down, especially in comparison to the other articles that came out on the same day."

Alissa swallowed, unsure of what to say. Had people really not liked it at all? She thought the headline was catching. Stanley had her rewrite it enough times. At least everyone agreed that a great headline was hard to write, so she wasn't the only one who struggled.

"And unfortunately, I was reading over the draft of the article on that music industry conference and it isn't hitting the mark either." Stanley sighed through his nose, looking down at his hands.

"Oh, okay. I'm happy to put in as much work as you need me to," Alissa said. "In what way did I miss the mark?"

The idea of putting in even more edits made her heart sink. It wasn't that she believed she was above criticism. Every writer was better with an editor. It was just that there was a big difference between needing to make some tweaks to an article, a feat she hadn't achieved in ages, and missing the mark. Missing the mark meant rewriting almost the whole thing from scratch.

"It was a little too small." Stanley gestured with his hands, as if the article were literally tiny. "Too focused on the individuals and not the big picture. The epic aspects of it, for lack of a better term. It needs to show how big the industry is."

"Right." The lump in Alissa's throat grew. "I'll fix it over the weekend."

"There's no need for that." Stanley took a deep breath and said, "I don't believe you're a good fit for *Epic* anymore, so we can hand it over to someone else."

Alissa blinked several times, trying to absorb what he'd just said. She understood the words individually, but collectively, her brain couldn't process them.

"I'm not a good fit anymore?" she asked, her voice small.

"No. I believe you'll do better elsewhere, but we'll have to end our relationship with you and let you go." Stanley's features softened. The rare sight made Alissa feel even more detached from the reality of the situation. "I'm sorry. I'll send over the details of your severance package right now."

Alissa still couldn't speak, but the finality of Stanley's apology told her that the conversation was over. She choked out an "okay" and got up again. Any fight she had left had drained out of her long before he called her into his office. What would arguing with him about her job do anyway? He had made up his mind and he wasn't a man who went back on his decisions. It was done.

"Have a good weekend," Stanley said as she walked out the door.

"You too," she replied, a reflex more than an honest sentiment.

Alissa would have laughed if she hadn't lost the ability to feel anything at all. How was she supposed to have a good weekend? Well, pretty much every day was like a weekend now that she didn't have a job. And the thought of looking for another one wore her out before she even started. If she couldn't make it at her dream job, what hope did she have for a job anywhere else?

She walked out into the cold Denver winter, the blustery wind chilling her skin.

What was she supposed to do now?

CHAPTER TWO

Dane Taylor jiggled his computer mouse and scooted closer to his desk. He didn't need to be at the offices of *The Outlet*, the newspaper he was starting in Blueberry Bay, especially since it was the weekend.

But he didn't have much else to do on a Sunday morning. Most of the town was still asleep and he'd already visited one of the few places that was open, Tidal Wave Coffee. He hadn't made any friends, not that he had a ton back in his former home, New York City. Most of the time he kept to himself, kept his head down, worked. His Sundays back in the city were spent sitting around in his apartment, lazily making breakfast and reading.

The moment his computer was awake, he turned on some ambient noise to take the edge off the silence of the office. Blueberry Bay was quiet almost all the time, even at his newspaper's office near the center of town. A few cars slowly drove by, but that was the extent of the noise. The contrast between the little town he'd ended up in and New York City grew more and more stark every day.

There were restaurants and local businesses filling "downtown" as the locals called it, but they opened late and closed early. There wasn't much of a night scene either, not that he was the type to go out a lot back when he lived in the city. People took their time and made small talk with each other, not thinking about where they had to be. The latter was the hardest adjustment. Some days he felt like he was speed walking when in reality, everyone else was going at his or her own pace.

It was a much humbler new beginning than he'd hoped. If someone asked him to pinpoint where Blueberry Bay was on a map a few months ago, he wouldn't have been able to do it. It was tucked away in coastal Rhode Island, away from major cities and all the things he knew before. It was almost as foreign as another planet. He never imagined that he'd pay so little for a house that was twice as big as his apartment, or that his biggest day to day problem was trying to make a quick run literally anywhere because everyone liked to have pleasant chats that went on a little too long.

But that didn't mean he planned to take it easy. He couldn't turn off his work ethic if he tried.

He sighed, sipping his latte and opening his email. The coffee was great, at least. Tidal Wave Coffee was one of the first places he'd stumbled upon when he moved to Blueberry Bay and he'd become a regular almost instantly. At first he'd been startled by how friendly and willing to talk the young baristas were, but now he was somewhat used to their brand of friendly optimism.

Dane checked, then double checked that everything he had to do for opening day was in order, his heart fluttering in his chest. He had worked in the newspaper business for his entire career, so he wasn't afraid of making basic mistakes. But there was a lot riding on it for him personally, especially since he was the sole owner of the paper. That was one benefit of his previous job; he'd been paid well enough to start this business.

The thought of his old job made his delicious latte taste bland in his mouth. Even though he'd been gone for months now, the subject of it still unsettled him. He hadn't liked the way his boss, Alvin, was running things at the paper where he worked in the city—sloppy reporting slipped through the cracks to garner clicks and sales and the writers were worked to the point where they couldn't produce good work. Alvin, whose work Dane had admired when he first started working there, let everything go as long as it got clicks.

It drove Dane nuts. He spent evening after evening, fixing other writers' work without being compensated or even acknowledged. Some days he felt like the entire newspaper was resting on his shoulders. He expected the weight of responsibility for the paper's success a little later when Alvin made him co-owner of the paper, not while he was editor in chief.

And the more he saw of how Alvin ran the paper, the more he hesitated at becoming co-owner. Was he going to end up doing all of the hard work? Were the financials Alvin gave him even accurate, or was Dane going to inherit a huge mess? What if that was the reason why Alvin had chosen Dane—he knew that Dane was going to work as hard as he could no matter what. If the paper was in trouble, Dane would pull it out.

After reading one too many messy articles with a blatant factual error in the second sentence, Dane had snapped. There wasn't a gentle way to put it.

He'd marched into his boss's office and confronted him about it, loudly enough for the entire floor to hear.

Dane had let him have it, listing every last grievance he had with the direction the publication was taking. He had piled up his complaints in his mind for so long that he could rattle them off one by one without pausing to think.

But Alvin hadn't been fazed. He'd just sat there, watching Dane with his socked feet up on his desk. When Dane had finished his rant, Alvin had shrugged and said, "Well, okay. Thanks for telling me."

Even now, the anger at his indifference bubbled up in Dane's chest so quickly that he had to take a deep breath and close his eyes. In the moment, he had seen red and resigned.

By quitting, he'd blown his chances of becoming a part owner of the paper, a job that could have allowed him to make the changes he wanted. Maybe if he had played his cards right, he could have bought out his old boss's share of the company and made it his own.

He sighed, running his fingers through his vibrant auburn hair. Had the decision been rash? He'd find out soon if *The Outlet* failed. The thought made his stomach churn. He tried to get in with another big city paper, but news of his explosive exit had traveled fast. No one wanted to touch him, and he doubted that would change if he had a failed paper under his belt on top of his dramatic outburst.

News of his move to Rhode Island had already spread through his circle of former colleagues, including Alvin. An email from him sat in Dane's inbox, unopened, the notification taunting him. He could have deleted it, sure, but the curiosity was overwhelming. Was Alvin going to tell him how crazy he was? Or was he going to beg for Dane to come back?

Or maybe it wasn't even about Dane. Did Alvin have news about the old paper? Even though it had been a total mess when he left, Dane cared about his coworkers, as much as they thought he was cranky and mad all the time. He didn't want them to lose their jobs.

Dane took several gulps of his latte, hoping the caffeine would bolster his confidence and get rid of the bitterness that he couldn't shake. He switched tabs so his email wouldn't be right in front of him. Whatever Alvin said, it wasn't going to make him feel any better.

Blueberry Bay wasn't his dream home by any

stretch of the imagination, but it was a good enough place for a paper. It and the surrounding towns didn't have a newspaper, making it easy to set up and fill that need. Or at least he hoped it would.

It made sense for him. New York City had so much competition that starting a paper there wouldn't have been a good business decision, and it wouldn't have made sense in any city. He had grown up in the Midwest, but as much as he loved his parents, he didn't want to return there. So, he turned his attention to New England. When he looked up towns where he could restart his life and start a paper, Blueberry Bay checked the boxes. He hoped he'd feel the same way now that the paper was finally launching.

He looked out the window beside his desk, taking in the open field behind the office and the sand dunes far beyond that. Though he was taken by the beauty of it, he missed the rush of stepping onto the street into a flurry of activity the way he had back in New York. It was odd—he'd never felt lonely back in New York, but now he did. It was something about how friendly everyone was, how excited they were to see each other. Friends gathering for coffee, going on walks, all of it.

And he felt like an outsider. He was already

introverted enough that making friends was going to be difficult. But making friends in what felt like a completely foreign place was even harder.

The front door of the small office opened, revealing a woman humming happily to herself.

"Morning!" Josie Garner, Dane's secretary, greeted him. Her desk was directly outside of his office, so she didn't have to raise her voice to be heard. "It's freezing out, isn't it?"

"It is."

"Glad I have this coffee to keep me warm!"

She peeled off her fluffy pink hat, shaking out her long, white blond hair, and hung her coat up on the hook next to the door. Then, she got right to work. Her side was facing Dane and she had her face turned away as she rifled through her desk drawers, but Dane knew she had a pleasant expression on her face.

He was glad for it. She was far better with people than he was, and incredibly smart too. As much as he wanted to try to do everything on his own for the paper, he needed help. People were going to call and ask questions, and he didn't want them to be put off by his brusque attitude. Especially around here. He wasn't rude, but he was having a hard time adjusting to being outside of New York. The standards for politeness were a lot higher.

They worked in silence, the clacking of their keyboards filling the office. Eventually Josie stood, coming up to his door.

"Everything's ready for tomorrow," she said. "And people are excited too."

"Yeah?" Dane swallowed.

"Totally. I overheard people talking about it when I went to Tidal Wave, actually." She smiled, her brown eyes sparkling. "It'll be great."

Dane could only nod. He was glad someone was excited about it. All he could muster was a pit of worry in his chest. What if he failed? What if everything imploded around him? This paper was his plan B and he didn't have another backup to fall back on.

Alvin's email was still sitting in his inbox, unopened. What if it confirmed every doubt he had? He didn't want to find out.

CHAPTER THREE

Alissa adjusted her laptop so it wouldn't slide off her stomach and onto the floor. She was stretched out on her couch, still in her pajamas despite it being eleven in the morning, and going through job posting after job posting. Her transition from sitting at her desk, to sitting on her couch with her computer on her lap, to this, laying on her back with her head propped up enough to see her screen, was a good indication of how the job hunt was going—optimism sliding into resigned despair.

She groaned, rubbing one eye with the heel of her hand. The words on the screen were starting to swirl around and she had far too many tabs open. Her cover letters were starting to run together so much that she was afraid she was sending some to the wrong potential employers.. She put her laptop on her coffee table and sat up, stretching. What day was it anyway? Wednesday? No, Thursday.

It hadn't even been a full week since she lost her job and the days were already blurring into each other. She didn't blame herself, though. Each day had been the same—wake up, remember her failures, eat some leftovers from the night before, and job hunt until she got discouraged or tired. Rinse, repeat. The monotony of it made her feel useless. On the hardest days of her job at *Epic*, she had wished for days to lay around and do nothing. Now that she was forced to do it, she hated it. How was not working this hard? Her brain felt inert, like she was a robot being tasked with the most basic things—wake up, eat, sleep, apply for jobs.

She got up, tucking her feet into her slippers and taking the short walk to her tiny kitchen. Despite her abundant amount of time, the counters were cluttered and dirty plates filled the sink. The thought of tackling those was almost as terrible as continuing her job hunt, so she grabbed a bottle of chardonnay and poured herself a glass. Why not? Her eleven AM was the exact same as her eleven PM and all of the days bled into each other.

The buttery coldness of the chardonnay washed

over her tongue as she walked back to her spot on the couch. Instead of opening up another document to write yet another cover letter, she opened a new window and pulled up her favorite streaming site. She had been at it for a while and was more than ready for a break.

But before she could get into a show, her phone rang on the coffee table.

"Ugh, come on," she groaned.

It was her twin sister, Caitlin Market. She loved Caitlin, but they were polar opposites in most ways. Alissa wasn't looking forward to the inevitable judgment about her career failures when she picked up the phone. The conversation where Alissa had told Caitlin that she had lost her job hadn't gone well, and Alissa had only escaped because Caitlin had to hop off the line before she could really get into it. Better to get this conversation over with.

"Hey, Caitlin," Alissa said, clearing her throat. She hadn't spoken more than ten words in days.

"Hey. How's it going?" Caitlin asked.

"It's going. Just job hunting." Alissa closed her laptop and put it down again. "I haven't had much luck finding anything."

"Mm." Caitlin paused, shuffling something

around on her end of the line. "It's still early though. You've only been at it for a few days."

"I know. I meant that there aren't that many newspaper jobs period."

Caitlin sighed and Alissa braced herself for what was about to come next.

"There are always jobs outside of newspapers too," Caitlin said. "Maybe it's time to expand your search. Find something more practical. I'm sure your skills could translate well to a number of different jobs."

That was exactly what Alissa assumed Caitlin would say. She had always been the practical twin who had her life together—married at twenty-one to a kind man, co-owner of the restaurant she ran with her husband, mother to the greatest niece Alissa could ever have. Alissa just wasn't the same way. Things being too similar day to day chafed, and she liked working in such a fast paced field that didn't offer as much stability. And she was okay with that. Well, she was until her dreams were crushed.

Alissa dug her hand into her short curls, her fingers getting caught on a knot. She hadn't looked in the mirror for more than a brief moment in days, so her hair was undoubtedly a disaster.

"I know there are," Alissa said. "But I'm not ready to give up yet."

"Okay," was all Caitlin said.

"It's my decision, Caitlin."

"I know. I know."

"I should get back to it." Alissa swirled her wine in her glass. "Talk to you later."

"See you."

Alissa hung up, slumping into the back of the couch. Maybe Caitlin was right. If she was having trouble even finding listings for jobs at newspapers or magazines, the odds of her actually getting one of those jobs was even slimmer. Her work was pretty good by most standards but it was a competitive space and she hadn't measured up at *Epic*. Settling for any kind of job was becoming a bigger possibility by the minute, but everything inside her shoved that possibility into the back of her mind.

She sipped her wine and pulled her knees up to her chest, looking around her apartment. *Epic* hadn't paid all that much, so her apartment was tiny, the single bedroom barely big enough to be considered a bedroom. It didn't get much light either, especially at this time of year, making it gloomy even with all the lamps she'd brought in. And having been stuck inside for days, she was sick of it.

That was it. She needed some time away to sort things out. Some place with a beautiful landscape and a calm energy, maybe by the beach. Her severance package had given her enough to live off of for a while. Surely there was a place that fit that description perfectly.

Feeling invigorated for the first time since Friday, Alissa grabbed her laptop and looked up beachside getaways. Hundreds of search results popped up, so she narrowed it down. She was chasing the atmosphere, not necessarily the amenities, and luckily there were tons of small bed and breakfasts peppering the coast of New England that seemed like a good fit.

Some were too bare bones and too far from the beach for her tastes, while other ones were way outside of her price range. But then, the perfect option appeared and she gasped—Literary Stays. It was a B&B with a literary theme, right on the beach. The inside was perfect too, with built-in bookcases and nooks to curl up with a book and look out onto the scenery. And its prices were great.

She hopped up and grabbed her wallet to book a stay there. It was the perfect place to recharge and find the creative energy that had made her want to be a writer in the first place.

* * *

"Good afternoon!" one of the many cheerful young people who worked at Tidal Wave Coffee said when Dane walked in. "Your regular latte?"

"Yes, please," Dane replied.

"I'm on it!"

Dane noticed that the baristas usually made small talk with the guests as they made their coffee, but he never knew what to say. When was the last time anyone had made small talk with him in a situation like this? It had been so long that he wasn't even sure if he was able to do it. What if he burst the barista's bubble by not engaging in the right way? That was another issue with being a regular at places —every interaction had more weight to it since he'd have to see someone again the next day.

He held in a sigh. When was he going to adjust to living here? Some days he worried he never would.

He paid, tipping the barista a dollar since she always made a good effort, and waited in the tiny space at the end of the bar. A stack of copies of *The Outlet* sat below the shop's bulletin board. At least several people had grabbed copies. He took one for himself even though he'd personally read it from front to back at least three times before it went to press.

He had worked on it, writing a few articles and rewriting ones that weren't as strong. Josie had made sure that it went to press on time and looked great. And the staff writer he'd hired...well, he tried. More accurately, Dane worked with him, trying to get good work in round after round of edits.

Writers he'd worked with at the newspaper back in New York had called him a control freak, a title he couldn't deny, but he just wanted to put out the best possible product. The writer wasn't giving it to him. But what else could he do? The best writers weren't clamoring to move to tiny towns in Rhode Island, no matter how idyllic they looked.

"Here's your latte, Dane!" The barista slid a sea green cup across the bar to him.

"Thanks."

He took his latte outside. It was unseasonably warm for this time of year, though that meant it was just cold instead of bitterly cold. The shop had a small patio that was screened in and heated in the winter, the perfect place to have a warm drink. He had never minded the cold.

Dane found a seat across the patio from an older couple having tea and opened up the second weekly edition of the paper. He couldn't stop himself from sighing. The paper was... fine. Just fine. It did the basics of reporting, at least. This issue had stories on the new bike path that connected Blueberry Bay to the neighboring town of Whale Harbor, as well as some local happenings that his staff writer had scraped up from somewhere.

It was the only outlet for news in the area, hence the name, so they didn't have competition to compare themselves to. But he wasn't ecstatic to have his name on it. It didn't have that gripping nature to it, the kind of paper that you had to read and talk to people about. *The Outlet* wasn't going to be sparking many conversations.

"Hey there," a man said, stepping up to Dane's table.

Dane looked up. The man was tall with long, dark wavy hair that he had tied back in a knot. He had a surfboard under one arm and exuded the confidence of a successful business owner. Even though Dane didn't know his face, he guessed this was Michael, the owner of the coffee shop. He had been a professional surfer and extended his love of the sport to the theme of his cafe.

"Hi," Dane said in return. "Are you Michael O'Neil?"

"I am. And you must be Dane Taylor." Michael smiled, the kind of smile that could win over even the grumpiest person.

"I am." Dane's brow furrowed as he shook Michael's hand. "Have we met before?"

"No. I figured it was you by your clothes." Michael nodded toward Dane's outfit. "Not in a bad way, of course."

Dane looked down at his dark green sweater, which was over a crisp dress shirt and slacks. Even though he had been in Blueberry Bay for months, he couldn't shake his habit of dressing up for work. The locals here were casual through and through, even at work. Michael was the perfect example—he was wearing a well-loved cable knit sweater and jeans with sneakers.

"That's not a bad thing to be known for, I guess." Dane shrugged.

"Well, you're more known for the newspaper, I'd say." Michael rested the surfboard against the wall and tucked his hands into his pockets. "It's been the talk of the town. A lot of people have been picking up copies. We're glad you started it."

"That's good to hear."

"Yeah. It's a good way for us to connect with the

other towns in the area," Michael said. "The paper looks great too."

"Thanks."

Dane bit back his next series of questions—did people actually like it, or were they more excited about the novelty of it? Was there anything going on in this town? If there was, how could he find it? It felt like the whole area was stuck in a loop of mundane happenings that weren't worth noting.

Now that Dane thought about it, Michael was a great choice for the front page. Everyone seemed to like Tidal Wave Coffee and Michael's history as a surfer was probably interesting. But everyone around here probably knew about him if news traveled the way Michael had described.

Dane bit the inside of his cheek, mentally kicking himself. When he chose Blueberry Bay for the newspaper, he thought he'd found the perfect hole in the market. But now that he was in town, he realized that the hole might have been there for a reason.

Dane wasn't sure if it was just his writer's research abilities or not, but the local stories he'd pulled up became duller the more he thought about them. He'd written about a new stop sign at a "busy" corner that was throwing off several locals, some whale sightings, and a horse that got loose and ran into the street for five minutes before he was caught.

Was that the most the town had to offer? Surely it wasn't. He didn't believe anyone would choose to live in such a dull place. But his writer knew the area way more than he did, so Dane had to trust him that this was truly the news of the area. It was either that or things that everyone already knew. In a town so small, could anything truly be surprising? How was he supposed to create news with a subpar writer and nothing going on?

He had to do something. He wasn't one to wait around and have someone else solve his problems.

"It's been nice chatting with you," Dane said, getting to his feet. "I've got to get back to the office."

"Nice chatting with you as well." Michael shook Dane's hand again. "Talk to you later."

CHAPTER FOUR

Blueberry Bay was perfect, even better than the images Alissa had seen online. She wasn't sure when check-in was at Literary Stays, so she'd come here to explore for a while. The B&B was technically located in Whale Harbor, a small town very close to Blueberry Bay, and although Alissa was sure she would explore that town at some point as well, there were plenty of beautiful views to keep her occupied in Blueberry Bay.

The main strip was along the water, lined with businesses, each one with a hand-painted sign out front. There was a small grocery store called Sandy's, a souvenir stand, a plant store, a comfort food restaurant that she absolutely had to try, and more. Signs pointed to the path to the beach and the boardwalk, which she gladly strolled along, even with her luggage. Then, she looped around when she reached the end, going back onto the main strip. A blue-painted building with a red crab painted on its sign greeted her first, the scent of hot, delicious bread wafting toward her.

Her stomach growled. She had left Denver early and hadn't wanted any of the overpriced, lackluster offerings at the airport. Now she was glad she'd saved up her appetite. The burly-looking men dressed in coveralls who were gathered at the picnic tables outside despite the cold seemed very satisfied with their meals.

Alissa walked inside, the warmth enveloping her.

"Welcome to The Crab!" the young woman behind the counter said with a smile. "Have you been here before?"

"I haven't." Alissa looked up at the chalkboard menu on the wall. "But I'm glad I passed by."

"I'll give you a second to look over the menu, then."

Alissa's stomach growled as she debated between several delicious options. A classic bacon, egg, and cheese, or the sandwich called the Dock, which had sausage, spicy red pepper jam, and eggs on a freshly made baguette?

"I'm ready," Alissa said to the young woman. "I'll try the Dock and a small coffee, please."

"Excellent choice!" The young woman punched her order into the cash register and Alissa paid. "We'll have that right up for you!"

Unlike the men outside, Alissa wasn't going to sit in the cold. She chose a seat in the corner where she could see out onto the street beyond the picnic tables.

The pace here was pleasantly slow, even on a Monday. If she were still working at *Epic*, she would have spent the last hour pushing her way through her freezing cold commute and standing in line to get a cup of terrible coffee. Then she would have trudged upstairs to her office, only to sit in front of the computer screen, frustrated that words weren't coming out.

This was much, much better on every level. The coffee was smooth with notes of chocolate and cherry, the kind of morning pick-me-up that she could get addicted to.

"Here you go!" The young woman dropped off Alissa's sandwich, which was in a red basket and partially wrapped in white butcher's paper.

"Thank you! It smells so good." Alissa pulled a few napkins.

"Enjoy!"

Alissa dug into her sandwich, holding back pleased sighs when the flavor hit her tongue. The combination of the spicy red pepper jam with the creamy yolk of the fried egg would have been phenomenal, but the addition of the house-made sausage made it the best sandwich she'd ever had in her life.

She polished it off and was already thinking of ways to come back to this place again. Literary Stays was one town over in Whale Harbor, but they were so close by that it was easy to get back by bike.

"That was the best sandwich I've ever had," Alissa said to the young woman as she put her basket in the stack next to the trash can. "Hands down."

"Really?" The girl beamed. "I'm so glad to hear that. Dad, did you hear that?"

"Hm? Did I hear what?" A man peered his head into the doorway that led to the kitchen.

He was older and rough around the edges, like he did a lot of manual work, but Alissa couldn't help but notice his strong jaw and handsome features under his rough stubble. If he got cleaned up, he'd be very distinguished.

"The Dock is the best sandwich that..." The young woman paused as if to ask for Alissa's name.

"Alissa."

"The Dock is the best sandwich that Alissa has ever had." The girl's smile made her look even more like a fairy from one of the books Alissa's niece Pearl loved so much—petite, with skin as fair and hair as dark as Snow White's.

"Glad to hear it," the man said with a nod before disappearing into the kitchen again.

"I'm Hannah, and that's my dad, Willis Jenkins." Hannah extended her hand over the counter. "He owns the shop."

"Nice to meet you." Alissa shook her hand. "I'm so glad I stumbled on this place."

"You're visiting from out of town, I'm guessing?" Hannah asked.

"I am. From Denver."

"Cool, welcome to Blueberry Bay! I've always wanted to visit Denver." Hannah chuckled. "Although maybe not at this time of year."

"Yeah, it can get cold during the winters. Although it's a fun place to be if you like winter sports." Alissa shrugged, sipping her coffee. "It's been so nice and quiet here so far."

"This is a great spot to get away from a lot of noise. Usually we get more tourists in the summer months. There are a few festivals and the beach is gorgeous around that time. The water's actually not freezing."

"Yeah. I just needed some time to figure out what I'm going to do next," Alissa said. "The place where I'm staying over in Whale Harbor is literary themed and near the beach, so it felt like the perfect place for me."

"That sounds super cute. And Whale Harbor is nice too," Hannah said. "Are you a librarian?"

"No, I'm a writer. For a newspaper. Or rather, I used to write for a newspaper." Alissa's cheeks warmed and she checked her watch.

"I can't wait to see Literary Stays. I'm not sure what check-in is like since it's this early."

"It wouldn't hurt to drop by. The bed and breakfasts around here aren't like big hotels." Hannah shrugged. "They're pretty relaxed with check-in times and things like that."

"True." Alissa pulled her coat back on. "I think I'll head over there now. I'll definitely be back soon."

"Looking forward to it! See you soon!"

Alissa hailed another cab, which took her the short ride to Literary Stays. The bed and breakfast was even more quaint than it appeared online, its pale blue and white exterior a nice complement to the sea next to it. There was a wraparound porch with a swing in the front and on the side facing the ocean, with views of the grasses and wilderness around it.

Alissa paid and thanked the cab driver, then got out. The clean, salty air blew her hair around as she walked up the porch steps. Now that she was closer, she noticed a few nods to some of her favorite authors—a plaque on the porch swing with a Jane Austen quote, a portrait of Oscar Wilde visible through the window, and a set of leather-bound books with painted pages in the windowsill.

Alissa knocked and waited, hoping she wasn't disturbing anyone. But the door opened moments later, revealing a smiling woman in an outfit so stylish that she looked like she'd walked off a magazine cover.

"Good morning!" the woman said, pushing her oversized, yet stylish glasses up on her nose. "Are you checking in today?"

"Good morning! Yes, that's me. Sorry for coming early if check-in isn't until noon."

The woman waved her hand and chuckled. "No worries at all. We're much more relaxed than big hotels. You're welcome to come right in and enjoy the atmosphere for as long as you'd like. I'm Monica Watson, the owner."

"Nice to meet you."

Monica stepped back and held the door open for Alissa. The comforting scent of books hit Alissa first and she took a deep inhale through her nose. It was bright and airy, with plenty of plush, comfortable seating and side tables for cups of coffee or tea to enjoy while reading. To their right was a picturesque winding staircase, a chandelier with what appeared to be intricately folded paper dangling in its center.

"Let me show you up to your room, then I can give you an official tour," Monica said.

Monica led Alissa upstairs. The second floor was lined with several doors, each one with a number and a small portrait of an author underneath. They stopped at the door at the end of the hall, which had a stellar view of the ocean beyond the trees.

"Here we are!" Monica unlocked the door and pushed it open. "This is the Jane Austen room."

Alissa couldn't stop her smile from growing. It was perfect. Since it was a corner room, there were two walls with windows, letting in plenty of natural light. There was even a bench along the sea-side window so she could curl up there and read or watch the sunset.

"It's gorgeous. I love it," Alissa said, tucking her rolling suitcase next to the desk.

"I'm sure you'll love the rest of the house too."

Monica led them out of the room, her honey blonde ponytail swinging. They went downstairs, then to the other side of the house. Monica showed off the backyard, which had a few picnic tables for warmer months, a gathering room, the kitchen where all the meals were served, and more.

"Do people live in this room?" Alissa asked as she gaped at the final room, the library. "Because I might."

It was a library out of a dream—big, floor-to-ceiling bookcases with a rolling ladder to reach the higher shelves, a big fireplace in front of several arm chairs, and a bar with a coffee machine, kettle, and mugs on the opposite side.

"It's our most popular room," Monica said. "And my personal favorite, but don't tell that to the library in town. I'm the librarian there."

"Your secret is safe with me." Alissa laughed. "I'll have to visit the library in town, though."

"It's worth a visit! I'd be happy to show you around there too." Monica straightened up a bust of one of the Bronte sisters that was sitting on a lower shelf. "It's a great library, but I wanted this to feel like a home too."

Monica's smile was warm and infectious.

"You've done a great job with the place." Alissa gazed up at the bookshelf again. "It's a book lover's dream. How long have you owned it?"

"Just a few months," Monica said. "I wish I had done it sooner, though. I was waiting around for something to happen, but one day I just went for it. Everything in my life changed, and I haven't looked back."

"Wow." Alissa found Monica's words comforting. She hoped she'd find her direction on this trip.

"Are you here to get away from the city for a while?" Monica asked.

"Pretty much. I just needed a break to figure things out since I got let go from my job and this seemed like the perfect spot. I'm a writer and love books." Alissa shrugged. "I need a change of scenery."

"Ah, I understand." Monica suddenly perked up. "You know what? This guy from New York City just started up a publication over in Blueberry Bay. It's not far from here."

"I was just there this morning." Alissa smiled. "It was lovely."

"Isn't it? You should talk to him about open

positions on his writing staff. I think it's called *The Outlet*."

"Oh, I don't know. I'm just visiting to sort myself out and figure out what's next." Alissa let out a nervous laugh.

"Of course." Monica nodded in understanding, right as the phone rang. "Oh, excuse me. I should get that. Just let me know if you need anything else to settle in!"

"Thanks!"

Alissa made her way up to her room with Monica's suggestion still floating through her mind. Maybe it was worth checking out, at least. What was left for her in Denver, anyway?

CHAPTER FIVE

Dane fought off another yawn, wondering if the barista had made his mid-morning latte with decaf. It was barely two in the afternoon and all he wanted to do was go to sleep. He had never felt this exhausted before, even during the most stressful times of his career.

Then again, he hadn't needed to try to create news out of thin air back then. He hadn't had to do four people's jobs at the same time. And he was excited to get up and go to the office every day back then. Now he just had a pit of dread in his gut when he woke up, a pit that only got deeper the more and more the day went on.

He sighed, squeezing the bridge of his nose and

turning his attention to the task he'd been putting off all day—reading an article from his staff writer.

The sliver of hope Dane had cultivated disappeared after reading the first three bland, lifeless sentences. When the writer had come to Dane with the idea for a story about a beach clean-up led by local high schoolers, Dane thought it had potential. From what he could tell, people around here liked feel-good stories about helping each other out. Apparently having a topic that people in town would love wasn't enough to make an article grab his attention.

"Shoot," Dane murmured to himself. Was it worth rewriting? It just wouldn't do. It was supposed to be the lead article of the week, one of two on the front page.

"Hey there!" Josie said, knocking on the door and holding up a bag from The Crab and a travel carrier of coffee. "I brought you a late lunch."

"Thanks." Dane pushed his keyboard away to make space for his food.

"How's it going?" she asked.

"Terrible." Dane scoffed, pulling his sandwich out of the bag. "This article is stale, so now I have to rewrite this one plus a few others. And I'm wondering if it's even worth rewriting or if I should just scrap it all together."

"Oof." Josie shook her head, sitting down across from him and sipping her coffee. "I've been trying to advertise for new writers but no one's responded yet. I posted online and at every store or shop that has a bulletin board."

Dane sank into his seat. Even the deliciousness of his Reuben couldn't distract him from that bad news. He figured someone would at least try to apply, even if they weren't a perfect fit.

"Does it matter?" he asked, opening his coffee to add more sugar to it. "I highly doubt that a small town like this would have anyone qualified to produce the kind of writing I'm looking for. And I refuse to compromise."

Josie nodded, though Dane could see her holding back something.

"What?" Dane raised an eyebrow.

"Maybe the town will surprise you. You never know." Josie shrugged, taking a long swig of coffee.

Dane couldn't muster up the hope that Josie had. All he could muster was energy to eat.

Maybe this was all a big mistake. How could he have assumed that other places would have the same well of talent as a big city? What if they searched for months until the paper had to close down? He shoved that thought aside right away. The idea of failure was too much to bear.

Alvin's email was still sitting in his inbox, untouched, and for whatever reason, the urge to open it came through in moments like this. Was he hoping that Alvin had changed his mind, or did he just want to linger in his misery a little more? Dane hoped it wasn't the latter. That wasn't like him. He fought until he got things done, and done well.

The front door of the office opened a little, then all the way, revealing a tall young woman standing with her hands tucked into her pockets. The light lit up her short curls like a halo around her head until she stepped all the way inside. Dane frowned. No stranger would be able to stroll into his office back in New York. That was yet another thing about this small town—it was so easy for people to show up like this.

"Um, hi," the woman said, hiking her canvas tote bag up on her shoulder. "Sorry, is this *The Outlet*?"

"It is! How can I help you?" Josie asked with a smile.

"Oh, good!" The woman brightened, her naturally pretty features becoming even lovelier. "I'm Alissa. I saw that you were looking for a journalist and wanted to see if the spot was still open."

Dane held in a sigh. This woman had amateur written all over her—her bright, excited expression, her eagerness. She probably still had dreamy thoughts of tapping away on a keyboard and chasing down a story like Lois Lane.

"The position requires someone highly qualified," Dane said. "And I doubt that'll be found around here."

Dane hadn't intended to sound so blunt, but his words came out that way anyway. Instead of being put off, Alissa straightened up, her combat boots squeaking on the wood floor.

"I'm not from around here. I'm from Denver," Alissa said. "I used to work for *Epic*."

Dane crossed his arms over his chest. He could admit he was slightly—*slightly*—impressed. *Epic* was a well-known publication and had some great writers. He had several stacks of back issues piled up in his living room, and sometimes he returned to them when he wanted to revisit a particularly inspiring article.

But instead of saying that, all Dane said was, "Okay."

"What kind of writers are you looking for?" Alissa asked, a tinge of annoyance in her voice.

"I need someone who can find the news that would be interesting to the people of the area and tell it in a compelling way. Talking to people, keeping your finger on the pulse, things like that," he said.

Alissa brightened even more, pushing her wire-rimmed glasses up on her nose. They were oversized in a way that was nerdy, but stylish. "That sounds right up my alley. I love talking to people and doing interviews."

Her earnest attitude was almost too much for Dane to handle. Was it really her speed? The articles *Epic* put out were the total opposite of what a town like this wanted. They were on the cutting edge of everything, while one of the most interesting articles that they'd published so far was about a traffic jam caused by geese in the middle of the main road.

A new fear popped into his head. He could begrudgingly admit that someone who worked for *Epic* wasn't going to drop into his office every other day. What if he got a great writer and then they left if they got bored? The idea of getting some great work, having the paper get a great reputation, then have that talent disappear... Dane couldn't let that happen.

"It's very different than *Epic*," Dane finally said. "In case you couldn't tell, this is a sleepy area and not a lot is going on. You won't have the same level of exposure or level of excitement."

"I know, but I know my strengths." Spots of color appeared on her cheeks. "I'm a great writer and I can get great stories out of people, no matter how small. Sometimes I prefer the smaller stories. They're more personal."

He believed that she was a great writer, but that was the problem—she seemed almost too good to be true. Dane wasn't that optimistic. Plus, that plucky attitude of hers was probably going to drive him nuts. She was positive now, but the glimmer in his eye told him that her attitude could turn a little sassy in the right circumstances.

Dane opened his mouth to speak, but Josie cut him off.

"Can you come in tomorrow so we can talk more specifics?" Josie asked. "Maybe around nine or so?"

"Of course!" Alissa's voice was bright, but the look she shot Dane was smug. "I'll bring my samples. See you tomorrow."

Alissa turned and left. Dane waited several beats before turning to Josie, who sipped her coffee, nonplussed.

"What on earth did you do that for?" Dane asked.

"Were you not just saying that things were going terribly and the articles were stale?" Josie asked. Dane huffed. "You need writers. And whether you want to believe it or not, that girl is really qualified and ready to work. You can at least try to give her a shot. Look at what she's written. Try."

Dane took a huge bite of his sandwich so he wouldn't have to answer right away. Josie, already able to read him more than he wanted her to, laughed.

"What, are you worried she's going to sass you or something? Or be insubordinate? Or maybe even make you smile?" Josie snorted, a smile spreading across her face. "Because that's exactly what you need—someone to resist you a little bit. Teach you how to deal with that kind of person. Give you a little contrast in your day."

Dane finished chewing and swallowed, pretending to only casually acknowledge her words. But in truth, they gave him something to think about for the rest of the afternoon. He considered himself to be tough, but Josie's words stuck out in his head—working with Alissa might teach him how to work with someone who contrasts him. He always thought he worked with people who contrasted him plenty. They were more upbeat than him by far and subtly let him know that fact regularly through passive-aggressive emails.

How much more contrast could he possibly need? He contrasted Josie. He contrasted everyone else in this town. Everything he did contrasted.

He waited until Josie had gone home for the day to open up his personal email. Now the email from Alvin sat below an email from a friend he hadn't heard from in a while, Ross. They used to work together at Dane's former paper, but Ross had moved on somewhere else. He hadn't heard from Ross in a while, so he opened the email.

Hey, Dane,

Hope you're all settled in Rhode Island. Remember when you told me that you were moving to Blueberry Bay and starting a paper, and my first question was, "where on earth is that?" Well, as it turns out, my girlfriend's family is from a town near there and we're coming to visit in a few weeks. I'd love to grab a beer and see what your paper looks like, if you're free.

-Ross

Dane's stomach clenched. In most circumstances, he would have been happy to see

Ross. He was a good guy and one of the few people he could call a friend, even if they didn't speak all that often. But the thought of him coming and seeing a failing paper was the last thing he wanted to experience.

So he had to make it work. He didn't want anyone to see him fail, or in the middle of failing.

Dane went ahead and emailed him back, saying he'd be happy to grab a beer. After he hit send, he sat back and sighed. Hopefully Josie was right—Alissa might have been just what the paper needed. Dane really needed her to be.

CHAPTER SIX

Alissa pulled the thick blanket around her shoulders and curled one leg underneath her on the porch bench. It was chilly out, but not unbearable with the heat lamp nearby. She wanted the crisp, salty air of the ocean against her skin. It was perfect with the beautiful view of the ocean, lit up by the full moon, and the sound of the waves crashing against the shore.

She had slept better than she had in ages since she'd arrived. There wasn't any street noise or strange creaks from her neighbors above and next to her. Just this—the ocean and the breeze. Monica's incredible food helped too. Tonight was cottage pie with pinot noir, followed by pecan pie for dessert. Monica and her husband, Braden, were great company too. Since Alissa was the only boarder at the moment, dinner felt like an evening with close friends.

Alissa smiled, opening the notebook she'd brought outside with her. She had written so much in the past few days that her hand was a bit sore. Her imagination had gone wild since she'd gotten here and she was adding onto notes for a romance novel she'd had an idea for years ago.

Everywhere she went inspired her—the cute elderly couple holding hands on the beach, the sight of boats drifting by, the smell of books that permeated the entire house. She hadn't been this creative and productive in years.

"This seems like a night for hot cocoa," Monica said, opening the door. "Would you like some?"

"That sounds lovely, thank you."

Monica disappeared again for a few moments, then reappeared with two mugs in hand. Alissa picked up her notebook and moved it so Monica would have a place to sit. The hot cocoa was thick and creamy, like melted chocolate, with a big, homemade marshmallow in the middle.

"What are you working on?" Monica asked.

"A romance novel I started years ago. Well, notes for one." Alissa thumbed through the pages, letting the cover close with a quiet *thump*. "It's been so picturesque here that I've been bombarded with ideas. The setting of the book is just like this town, oddly enough. I didn't plan it that way. I already feel like I want to stay here longer than I thought, just because my creative juices are flowing."

"That's great!" Monica brought her mug to her lips.

"Yeah. And I went to Blueberry Bay to ask about that job at *The Outlet*." The pleasant vibe she'd cultivated between dinner and sitting outside faded.

Memories of Dane's annoyed face stood out starkly in her memory. What was his deal? She had come in trying to fix a problem that he had and he acted like she had been bothering him.

"Good for you! How was it?"

"It was... kind of rough." Alissa let out a breath through her nose. "The publisher—Dane is his name, though I only found that out from the name plate on his desk—was weirdly not thrilled that a qualified writer came strolling through the door."

"What? Why?" Monica's brow furrowed. "No offense, but the paper really needs some good writers."

"I don't know. It would be amazing if it worked out but Dane is..." Her cheeks warmed.

"Disagreeable. He would be even more handsome if he smiled like, ever."

Alissa's face heated even more. She hadn't intended for her impression of his looks to slip out, but it was true. Dane was undeniably handsome. His stylishly cut auburn hair, strong jaw, and vibrant green eyes made Alissa's heart skip a beat. Then he balanced that out with that grumpy attitude of his.

"Oh, even more handsome?" Monica nudged Alissa with her shoulder. "Do you like him deep down?"

"Goodness, no. I don't even know him." Alissa adjusted the blanket on her shoulders. "And besides, he might not be my problem. I don't know if I'll even get the job."

Though if she were being honest with herself, she hoped she would. From the way Josie had spoken and how long the listing she had found online had been up, they needed someone and she was more than qualified to be that person.

CHAPTER SEVEN

Alissa straightened her skirt, then her collared shirt for the fifth time since she'd arrived outside of the offices of *The Outlet*. Her hair was somewhat of a lost cause, though she'd tried to tame her curls before she left. They weren't agreeing with her or each other, spiraling all over her head.

Her heart was pounding out of her chest. She looked presentable enough for an interview. Sure, her hair was a little bit out of control, but her outfit showed she cared about making a good first impression. Her writing was what mattered anyhow, and she was confident that her samples and resume would impress Dane.

Alissa took one more deep breath and opened

the door to the office. Dane's office door was closed, but Josie was sitting at her desk.

"Good morning!" Josie said, standing up. Her white-blond hair was up in a braid that wrapped around her head, a look Alissa loved but could never pull off with her curls. "I'll let Dane know you're here. You can have a seat right here."

"Thank you."

Alissa sat down on the lone chair next to the door while Josie went to get Dane. She spoke to him in hushed tones for a moment before closing the door again.

"He'll be ready shortly," Josie said, sitting back down at her desk.

Alissa fidgeted with her bag and her glasses, Josie's typing filling the room.

"Is he always as cranky as he was yesterday?" Alissa asked when the silence got to be too much.

Josie gave Alissa a knowing smile. "He has a lot of resentment built up about moving here from the big city and trying to get this paper off the ground when it's a sleepy little place. But he's less cranky and more... passionate, I guess is the word. He just wants things done well."

Alissa nodded slowly, taking in what she'd said. She was used to working with people who wanted things done right. If the articles he wanted were anything like he'd said—interviews and finding the small, personal stories of those who lived in the area —then she knew she could meet his expectations.

A few moments later, the door to his office opened. Alissa thought that she dreamed up how good looking he was in some nerves-related hallucination, but no, he really was as good looking as she remembered. As he was the day before, he was dressed in a button-down shirt, the sleeves rolled up, a tie, and slacks. His auburn hair was a bit messy, like he had been running his fingers through it. The florescent lighting didn't flatter most people, but Dane wasn't most people. His vibrant green eyes caught in the light as he studied Alissa.

"I'm ready," he said, turning on his heel.

Alissa got up and followed, shutting the door behind her. Every ounce of self-consciousness she'd had outside the office came rushing back as she sat down across the desk from Dane.

"Your samples?" he asked, hardly looking up at her.

Well, then. Alissa ignored his curtness and pulled her samples out of her bag. That attitude took away from his attractiveness, at least a little. And that made her much less nervous at first. It wasn't like they were starting at a great point and spiraling downward. Dane read the samples in silence, taking his time. She resisted the urge to fidget.

"The first article is a favorite of mine," she blurted. "The one on the boat company. I went down to a shipbreaking yard and watched them take apart some old ships. It was fascinating. And the scrap metal is apparently a big business for them."

Dane glanced up at her for a moment, then looked back down. "I see."

He didn't say anything more—he just went back to reading. Alissa tried to analyze every micro expression on his face. Was he disappointed? Interested? He didn't seem disappointed, at least not yet. But the silence was so deafening that she worried he was let down by what she'd brought in.

"Do you have any questions for me?" Alissa asked.

"I'm not done yet."

Alissa folded her hands between her thighs so she wouldn't pick at a thread on her cardigan or do anything distracting. Finally, Dane sat back in his seat. The tension around his eyes and mouth that Alissa had become accustomed to was gone. If she wasn't mistaken, he looked impressed. Then he quickly hid it behind his cool exterior again.

"These are good samples," he said.

"Really?" Alissa asked, sitting up. An evening's worth of anxiety melted right off her shoulders.

"Yes." Dane slid her samples across the table again. "But you don't live here, do you?"

"Nope, not right now, but with the way things are going here, it seems like I'm worth a shot." Alissa couldn't help but grin.

"I'll give you a chance, then," he said, as if this gave him a very minor headache. "It won't hurt to give you a try."

Alissa held in an enthusiastic *yes*. "Thank you so much. I'm really excited to get started."

"Josie will let you know about your payment and your hours," he said, turning back to his computer.

Alissa thanked him again and left to talk to Josie. And when she walked outside, she finally let out the excited sound she'd been holding in. Even if she had to work with a grump, at least he was a grump who liked her work.

CHAPTER EIGHT

Caitlin peeked into her daughter Pearl's bedroom one more time to make sure she was asleep. Thankfully, Pearl was well past the phase of refusing to go to bed. Then, Caitlin shut the door quietly. She padded down the carpeted hallway to the living room, where a glass of wine and some popcorn were waiting for her on the coffee table.

The room felt empty and silent, a sharp contrast from how it used to feel after she put Pearl to bed. A few years ago, she and her husband James would use this time to be together, catching up and watching TV if they didn't collapse into bed first. The room always felt like a warm, comforting bubble that was just for them. They would curl up next to each other, especially when the weather was cold, and talk about anything that came to mind.

Caitlin sighed and picked up the remote, looking around. Where was James, anyway? She spotted him in the kitchen, standing at the fridge and drinking something. Instead of inviting him over, she turned on the TV, unsure of what to say. She found a silly, over the top drama and settled in to watch.

A few moments later, James came in, his laptop in his arms.

"I'm going to do some work in the office, then head to bed," he said as he passed.

"Okay. Good night." She looked up at him and he placed a polite kiss on her cheek.

This was their norm now—a kiss on the cheek and zero time spent together once Pearl was in bed. But tonight felt different, somehow. More alone despite the TV playing in front of her. She wanted some of their old magic back. Not the new, fluttery feelings of infatuation, but the comfortable love they'd had—being able to talk about anything and everything, being excited to share her day with him. Being one hundred percent comfortable with him.

She sighed, taking a delicate sip of her wine. At least they weren't arguing like they were for a while. But then again, maybe the silence was worse. A sign that they were drifting apart after six years of marriage. Dread filled her chest, then cooled with resignation. This was just something that happened to people. They had their business, a thriving French restaurant, and Pearl, whose daily activities took up more and more time now that she was in kindergarten.

But knowing that this wasn't unheard of didn't make her any less upset about it.

Caitlin's phone buzzed on the table—it was Alissa, so she turned down the TV.

"Hey," Caitlin said when she answered.

"Hey!" Alissa sounded breathless, but in a happy way. "Guess what?"

"What?"

"I got a job writing for a paper here!" her twin said.

"Whoa, I thought you were just going to Blueberry Bay to escape for a while." Caitlin muted the TV entirely.

"I know, but Monica—she owns the bed and breakfast where I'm staying—said that she heard about open writer positions for this new publication, *The Outlet*. I figured it wouldn't hurt to check it out," Alissa said in nearly one breath. Her excitement radiated through the phone. "From what my boss, Dane, says, I'll be doing all of the things I like, like interviewing people and telling their stories. No big exposes on industries and canned answers."

"Do you think he'll be a nicer boss than Stanley?" Caitlin asked. Stanley had been a tough boss and Alissa had frequently talked to her about it.

"Ugh, that's the one downside. Dane's so grouchy," Alissa groaned. "His secretary, Josie, had to practically beg him to give me a shot. Can you believe that? He was dying for writers and he almost sent me packing."

"He sounds like a treat."

"I know. But he liked my samples a lot and I'll get to have more freedom over what I write." Alissa let out a dreamy sigh. "It's kind of perfect, really."

"That's great," Caitlin said, even though a stab of jealousy pierced her chest.

Alissa's life was chaotic and bohemian, which was far from how Caitlin liked to live. Caitlin's closet was filled with coordinating pantsuits, neutral high heels, and tailored blouses. Back when they were younger and shared a room, Caitlin's side was tidy while Alissa's was an explosion of books and papers.

But Alissa's life sounded exciting. And Alissa sounded happy for the first time in a while, and

Caitlin was far from it, not that she'd say anything in Alissa's happy moment.

"Are you going to move there?" Caitlin asked. "You just got fired and you were planning on visiting there for a week, not forever."

"I know. But it's so pretty and charming here. I'll just see how things will pan out," she said, her tone sure and steady.

* * *

Alissa's first day at work outfit was less rumpled than her regular choice of oversized sweater and linen pants, but it still wasn't as fancy as she'd liked. Dane dressed extremely well and Josie was casual yet stylish. But this outfit had to do—she needed to get going soon.

"Too late to change now," Alissa murmured to herself as she tried to tame her curls.

It was chilly enough that she needed a hat, but a hat plus her curls plus the wind was a bad combination. The YouTube tutorial she tried to follow was a complete disaster, making her look like she'd rolled off the set of a period drama, but not in a good way.

Finally she threw her hands into the air and

resorted to her usual style, loose and curling around her ears. Her dangly earrings, which she had gotten at a craft fair last summer, were the final touch that she needed. Not that it mattered. What was the point in looking good for Dane? He was her boss and he was too much of a scrooge to pay anyone a compliment.

She snorted at the idea of him saying something nice, even. Complimenting her samples was clearly like pulling teeth for him. She was glad that Stanley hadn't been the type to dole out loads of praise since Dane definitely wasn't going to do that.

Alissa went downstairs, the scent of a hearty breakfast drifting up to her nose. Back in Denver, she hadn't eaten a good breakfast on a regular basis. Most mornings she grabbed a granola bar and scarfed it down as she walked, or she just had a cup of coffee from the cart outside of her office. Monica's breakfasts had quickly changed that. The spread on the dining table made her mouth water—slow cooked oats with berries that Monica had frozen from last summer, cheesy scrambled eggs, crispy potatoes, and smoked salmon.

"Good morning, " Monica said, poking her head out from the door to the kitchen. "Help yourself—I'm making more coffee."

"Wow, this looks incredible." Alissa grabbed a plate from the sideboard and debated what to eat first. But now that she was thinking about actually eating, her stomach flipped in her belly.

But Monica had put in a lot of effort to cook, so Alissa plated up a little bit of everything. She sat down and Monica reappeared with a fresh pot of coffee.

"Are you excited for your first day?" Monica asked, filling Alissa's mug, then her own.

"So excited. Almost too excited." Alissa took a bite of the oatmeal, which was way too delicious for something healthy. It was thick, creamy, and just sweet enough. "All of this food is so good but I'm a little too wound up to eat."

"Braden and some of his crew are coming by later to eat breakfast, so it'll all get eaten." Monica chuckled, poking at her cheesy eggs. "They work up big appetites after getting off the water."

"Oh, good." Alissa smiled, tasting the smoked salmon with the potatoes. Braden ran his late father's fishing company, so there were often evenings when his employees would come over for dinner. Alissa loved hearing stories about their time at sea—she mentally filed away some of the turbulent emotions they had to tap into in her writing. "I'm not sure how much freedom Dane will give me, but I hope I can talk to some of the fishermen soon. I think some of their stories would be great for the paper."

"Their stories are great, aren't they?" Monica grinned. "Dane's lucky to have you. You're already thinking of great ideas and you haven't even had your first day."

"I can't wait to get started." Alissa laughed, her appetite returning.

"I know you'll do great," Monica said.

Alissa savored the rest of her breakfast. It was the perfect start to what she hoped would be a great day.

CHAPTER NINE

Dane's eyes drifted toward Alissa's new desk, which he could see from inside his office. She pushed her glasses up on her nose, then went back to typing, a small smile on her face. Her attention hadn't strayed from the task at hand since he'd given her when she came in the door.

He looked back at his screen at his own article. The assignment he'd given Alissa, a story on the reconstruction of a historical lighthouse, was much bigger than he would have given a beginner—there was a lot of research involved on a tight deadline. But he didn't have much of a choice at the moment. The lighthouse was some of the biggest news in the area and he had too much on his plate to do all the research and write the article in time.

Alissa's eager amateur attitude would get it done.

He got a few sentences down, but looked back at her before he could get out another. He hadn't wanted to think about it during her interview, but she was lovely in a very natural, pure way that he appreciated. She didn't wear any makeup, but her lips were a naturally lovely pink. She had the bottom one between her teeth, her brows furrowed in focus.

Even though her "eager to prove him wrong" attitude drove him a little crazy, it was actually charming in its own way. She wasn't just doing it to prove a point—she was doing it because she loved the work. And fine, he could admit to himself that she didn't write like an amateur, despite her attitude. Her writing was exceptional and took some of his fears that he'd have to show Ross a crumbling publication off his shoulders.

Still, he hadn't had the courage to open up Alvin's email. No, he needed to feel more secure in himself to do that. He wasn't sure why, though. Alvin hadn't been particularly intimidating when he worked for him, but the idea of Alvin tearing apart his paper when it was still in his infancy hurt. Dane didn't want to rock his own confidence when each day was still a struggle.

Dane's eyes drifted back to Alissa. She twirled

one of her short curls around a pen absently, like she did it all the time. Then, she brightened like a knot had just come undone and typed furiously.

Dane remembered being that excited about his job. Every article was an adventure and a puzzle for him to solve. Writing an article that did well and had an impact felt like winning a prize every single time. Every well-received article brought him closer to his byline being recognized the world over.

But now it was just this—sitting at his desk, grinding out words and worrying about all of the other things that went with publishing a paper. The romantic side of writing and caring for each word had been replaced with thinking about ad revenue and paper costs.

He sighed, wishing he could steal an ounce of Alissa's moxie.

"Hi there," Josie said, stepping into the doorway. The small smirk on her lips made his neck heat. He hadn't meant to stare at Alissa that long.

"Hi. What do you need?" Dane cleared his throat and rolled closer to his desk.

"Nothing." Josie's smile grew as she stepped into his office. She glanced over her shoulder, then leaned forward and whispered, "I think she's going to work out."

Dane shook his head. "It's easy to be enthusiastic. It doesn't mean anything if the article isn't good. I have to read her last article."

The first story he'd given her was much easier, more of a test than anything—he told her to report on a new surf shop opening up on the beach.

The short article had been sitting on his desk since yesterday and he hadn't read it yet. He wasn't sure why—was he afraid of it being underwhelming? Of her not working out, despite his open skepticism?

Josie shrugged, not put off by his skepticism. "Go ahead and read it, then. But I say she's a good choice."

The phone rang and Josie looked over her shoulder, heading back to her desk. Dane sighed and went into his email to find the article Alissa had sent.

He got up and shut the door to his office. He didn't want Alissa's excitement to distract him or sway his opinion on her work.

He sat down and read the article. It was... fantastic. She had taken a mundane business opening and turned it into something exciting by threading in quotes and observations of the people who were excited to shop there.

"Well, then," he murmured to himself, leaning

back in his leather chair. She had done a fantastic job. His mood lifted, just a tiny bit.

"I've been thinking about this all day," Alissa said, eyeing the sandwich in the red basket in front of her. It was another one of The Crab's specialties, a twist on a lobster roll with crab.

"I'm not even going to say I've overhyped it," Braden said with a smile. "It's my favorite sandwich in the world."

"He's not kidding," Monica said, sitting on the same side of the picnic table as her husband. "He's talked about it in his sleep before."

Alissa picked up the sandwich and took her first bite under Monica and Braden's watchful gaze. Flavor exploded on her tongue, followed by a perfect combination of textures. The fresh bread was the perfect vessel from the creaminess of the crab salad tucked inside. Her face must have been lighting up because Monica and Braden's did too.

"This is amazing," Alissa said after she swallowed. "I'm going to be dreaming about this too."

"Loving the crab roll?" Hannah asked, coming

out of the restaurant with three blue cocktails on a tray.

"I'm already in love with it and I've had two bites," Alissa said.

"I'm glad to hear it!" Hannah smiled. "Here are three cocktails on the house. The perfect companion to this gorgeous sunset."

"Thank you!" Monica accepted her cocktail from Hannah. "What's in them?"

"I call them the Ocean Breeze." Hannah put down the last two cocktails. "They're coconut rum, pineapple juice, blue curaçao, and coconut water."

"Sounds delicious. Thank you, Hannah," Braden said.

"My pleasure!"

Once Hannah left, Monica raised her glass. "To Alissa's new job!"

"Cheers!"

They tapped their glasses together and sipped the drinks. Hannah was right—they were the perfect complement to the sunset view. Even with the chill in the air, the edge taken off by the heat lamps around them, the cocktail made it feel like summer.

The three of them dug into their crab rolls and house-made chips, taking the edge off their hunger.

"So, since the job seems permanent, what are

you going to do about staying here?" Monica asked, wiping her fingers with a napkin. "I thought you were only here temporarily."

"I'm not sure." Alissa shrugged. "I think I'll keep things as they are for now and see how the job goes before committing to a place."

"You're welcome to stay at the B&B for as long as you'd like," Monica said with a smile.

"I'm glad to hear that. I've had a great time reading in the library, but now I can write in there too."

"Working from home after your first day?" Braden teased.

"I know, I know." Alissa's cheeks flushed. "But if I put enough work in, I know I'll put *The Outlet* on the map around here."

Her voice trailed off when she saw Dane coming from inside. He had totally heard her, if his raised eyebrow was any indication. Her blush expanded from her cheeks to her whole body. It didn't help that he looked as handsome as he did. Instead of the tailored shirts and slacks he wore every day at the office, he was in a dark green flannel button down that played nicely against his auburn hair and dark jeans. They were still fancy, though, not at all like the worn flannel and work-frayed jeans of the locals.

To Alissa's relief, he didn't come over and make a fuss. He took his food and sat at another table, opening up a book.

Her embarrassment faded as she, Monica, and Braden went back to their food. They talked about some new books that Monica had gotten at the local library, which she had ordered more copies of for the house. The discussion about books led to a spirited friendly debate about book to movie adaptations and which ones were their favorites.

More people came outside as the evening went on, friends of Monica and Braden's too. They mingled from table to table like a party, introducing her to some of the people they knew. Everyone was as welcoming as Monica and Braden were, treating her as if she had been there for years.

Eventually they ended up talking to a few of their friends near Dane's table. Alissa couldn't avoid him anymore. A basket filled with sandwich crumbs and a few chips sat in front of him, along with a half-finished beer. The book he was reading was facedown, so Alissa couldn't tell what it was. But it was the thick, serious tome that she expected him to read in his free time.

"Hey," she said.

"Hi." Dane looked up at her, what passed for a

smile crossing his face—just a slight change around his eyes, the smile not reaching his mouth. “Celebrating your first steps on the journey to put *The Outlet* on the map?”

“Just pretend I didn’t say that.” Alissa wanted a hole to magically open up underneath her so she could get out of this. Or she wished she had access to a time machine to stop her past self from saying that.

But then she realized that he was actually joking. At least a little bit. His grass green eyes had an almost friendly shine to them, but then he blinked and it disappeared.

“The two articles you’ve written are really good,” he said.

Alissa couldn’t stop her grin from spreading.

“I’m glad! I had a lot of fun writing them. The people around here are so friendly.” Alissa rested her hand on the back of the chair across from him. “As you can see. Everyone’s been very welcoming.”

“Glad you had fun writing it,” he said. “It must be rewarding for you.”

His expression now and at work suggested that he had anything *but* fun writing.

“It doesn’t seem like you have a lot of fun at your job,” Alissa said softly.

Dane sipped his beer, looking out on the horizon.

It was dark now, but the lights around the outdoor seating area lit up the startling green of his eyes. The table was small, so she was close enough to see the freckles across his cheekbones and nose. They made him look a little bit boyish in a way that was a nice contrast to his gruff attitude.

"It's complicated," he finally said, an edge to his voice. "I never expected this little town to be the place where I'd start my first sole-owned newspaper. It's not exactly the center of the world."

"It doesn't have to be the center of the world to be worthwhile or exciting." Alissa shrugged, looking out onto the horizon too. "There's beauty to be found here, right? Look around. It's special in its own way."

She looked over her shoulder at all of the people gathered on the patio, laughing like old friends. This wasn't something she'd ever see back in Denver, or any other city where she'd visited.

When she looked back at Dane, he was studying her, an inscrutable look in his eye.

"Yeah, sure," he said, taking a swig of his drink. The edge in his voice had softened, just a touch.

CHAPTER TEN

"Morning!" the perky teenager behind the counter said to Dane when he walked into Tidal Wave Coffee Monday morning. "The regular?"

"Yes, please."

He gave the barista exact change, plus tip. Even though he had gone to the same big coffee chain day after day back in New York and he knew that they knew him, none of the baristas there ever greeted him as a regular.

To his surprise, he was starting to like it. Just a little, though. He hadn't tackled making small talk with them, but he was more comfortable with their attention and warmth than he was when he first moved to town.

The barista finished his latte and slid it across the

bar. Dane thanked her again and took his coffee, plus a copy of *The Outlet*, to a table under a heat lamp at the corner of the outdoor patio.

He sipped his latte—good as always—and opened up the paper. Alissa's article on the new surf shop was front page. Even though he had read it and edited the article, Dane reread it. Her words were even better in print. He wasn't afraid to admit that, at least to himself. She was an amazing writer.

Dane reread some other articles, getting so absorbed in them that he was startled by Michael's presence in front of him.

"Hey there," Michael said, running a hand through his wavy dark hair, which was loose around his shoulders today.

"Morning."

Michael sat down across from him with his coffee. This was still a little weird for him—having people come up to you in places like this. People in New York City ignored each other unless something dire was happening in front of them.

But Michael was treating him like he was a part of this town, not a guy from the big city who had just moved there. Dane appreciated it. As friendly as everyone was, sometimes he felt as if they were looking at him as Dane Taylor, the New

Yorker with the newspaper instead of just Dane Taylor.

Alissa popped into Dane's head against his will. She had been welcomed in like a local right away. Was it because of her warm attitude? Probably.

"I trust that latte's still as good as ever?" Michael asked.

"It is. It never fails to wake me up."

"Good." Michael smiled. "The paper is selling well."

"I'm glad to hear that." And Dane was glad that Michael wasn't just exaggerating. The sales numbers that Josie had put together showed that they didn't have to worry about shutting down at all.

"The article on that surf shop opening reminded me of something." Michael paused to drink his coffee. "I'd love for the newspaper to cover surfing events in the area. It would mean a lot. Some people don't even know there's surfing around here, much less events."

"Of course. That sounds great." Dane chuckled. "And no offense, but not a whole lot goes on here that qualifies as news, so I'd be happy to have something real to cover."

"No offense taken." Michael held up his hand. "Though to be fair, it seems like Alissa has done a great job at making news around here exciting. I read her articles and she did such a good job."

Michael spoke about her like they were old friends, not like Alissa was someone who had come to town for a vacation and ended up getting a job.

"I agree," Dane said. "She brings out the charm in the area and knows how to talk to people."

"She does. One of the people she interviewed is my surf buddy and he had nothing but good things to say about her. And he's usually not the kind of guy to be a talker in general. I almost want to ask her how she managed to get so much out of him," Michael said with a chuckle. His phone buzzed in his pocket. "Ah, I should probably get going. You should come catch some waves with me one of these days."

"Only if you're willing to put up with me falling off the board every five seconds."

"Everyone starts somewhere!"

Michael laughed and waved, disappearing inside. Dane suppressed a smile and pulled his phone out of his pocket, checking his email. He had a status update from Alissa, whose email had more than one exclamation point, and some administrative updates from Josie.

A text message burst through his focus—his mother.

JOHANNA: How are things?

That was all her text said. His thumbs hovered over the screen.

He didn't like to be dishonest, but his mother only wanted him to love what he was doing. Telling her how deflated he felt about his work was a guaranteed way to worry her. That was the last thing he wanted.

But then again, he had some hope too. Alissa had... inspired him with her enthusiasm.

He shook that thought off. No, she was overly optimistic. That would only lead to more misery for her in the future. She had to be realistic. That zeal was going to wear off and reality was going to take its place—not every article was going to be fun and she might have to deal with the business side of the paper at some point. She'd realize that soon enough. He didn't have to burst her bubble.

DANE: They're okay. Everything's just fine.

His mother's response bubbles popped up instantly. She was a slow texter, but he preferred that to her using speech to text to send an incomprehensible stream of words that took several seconds to parse.

JOHANNA: ***All right. But it's okay if you aren't okay, sweetheart.***

Dane suppressed an eye roll that would have made his teenaged self proud. He didn't blame his mother for her concern. He wasn't always the most forthright with how he was feeling, especially if it would make her worry more than she already did. But he was mildly annoyed that she assumed he wasn't doing well from a few simple texts.

He lifted his thumb to respond, but stopped. Was his mother sensing something that he was denying in himself? He *thought* he was okay. She knew more than anybody that he wasn't the type to walk around with a smile on his face.

Maybe life here was draining him in a different way than life drained him back in New York. Before, the small irritations in life—the late trains, the long lines, the inconvenience of something as simple as laundry—combined with his frustration at his boss's detachment made him collapse face first into bed every night.

But here, there wasn't any of that. The contrast between him and everyone else was what got to him. Even with how welcoming everyone was, he still felt like he was on the fringes looking in. Writing about the town wasn't making it any better, as he'd once assumed. It almost made him feel like an anthropologist reporting on another culture, not sinking in enough to truly be a part of it.

The closest he felt to belonging was when he read Alissa's pieces. She brought out the common threads between people and he could see how he wasn't all that different.

So maybe he wasn't okay after all, but it really was fine.

He saw better things on the horizon, especially with the paper and all the great things they could do with Alissa on board. Maybe it would feel like home soon enough.

CHAPTER ELEVEN

Instead of being awoken by a siren or a garbage truck, Alissa was awoken by the lack of noise. It was so still that her rustling the sheets felt excessively loud. For a moment she thought something was seriously wrong—Denver was never silent—but then she remembered where she was. Whale Harbor was almost Denver's polar opposite.

She sat up and rubbed her eyes, tapping her phone screen to check the time. It was five fifteen, way earlier than she needed to wake up. The barest hint of sun shined through one of the windows.

She leaned over and gasped. The sky above the trees was illuminated with the pale pinks, oranges, and blues of the sunrise, the dark outlines of the trees the only thing between her and the horizon.

She got out of bed and opened the curtains to get a better look. The way her Denver apartment was positioned hardly let light in, much less a full view like this. How was something as simple as a sunrise this stunning? Now she truly understood what the word "breathtaking" meant. Taking a photo wasn't going to capture the beauty of it, but she wanted to capture the feeling of looking at it in words.

Alissa sat down at the small desk in the corner, which still gave her a view of the sunrise, and pulled out her old writing notebook. She had hastily shoved it into her suitcase before she left the way she often did on the few vacations she took in the past. Usually it sat unused, but now she felt compelled to break it out.

She flipped through to find a blank page, passing by notes for a story she started years ago. The ideas were loose—all she had were the characters, including a moody, mysterious man with a troubled past.

She flipped back to them, smiling as she scanned her notes. Working at *Epic* had drained every ounce of her creative juice, so she had stopped working on it. But the more she read her notes, the more she saw ways to start it again. They were a bit of a mess, but a mess she could work with.

Her heart fluttered as she grabbed a pen. It had been so long since she'd written anything creative that she wasn't sure where to start. Since all of the writing she did these days was slated to be published in the paper, she thought about her book in print, sitting on the shelf of a book store. One of her college professors had told her that if she finished a book to send it her way. She'd happily help Alissa publish it.

The thought sent a rush through Alissa that was much stronger than coffee.

She threw on a thick cardigan and sweatpants, then took her notebook and pen out onto the porch of the B&B. The sunrise was even more spectacular from that vantage point, filtering through the tree trunks. She took a deep breath in. The combination of the sea salt air and the view was a balm on her soul.

She looked over toward the sea, the sky above it catching the light from the sunrise. The view from the boats was probably even better than this, the gentle rocking of the sea underneath. As much as she liked her view, she wanted to stand on the bow of a ship with a cup of coffee, soaking it all in.

That was it—her brooding main character had to be a fisherman. But what would make this mysterious man change?

She flipped open a new page and scribbled down a few notes, pausing with the end of the pen on her lips. The sound of the ocean cleared her head and gave her an answer—love. He'd see a beautiful siren while he was out on the water, standing on the bow of a ship with his coffee. And the siren, seeing something special in the fisherman, doesn't kill him as her kind usually would.

She wrote down more ideas as fast as her hand could manage. It was as if she had stopped writing the characters days ago, not years. They came to life as the sun rose and the world woke up. Monica appeared with a cup of coffee for her, but left Alissa to her writing.

Alissa's phone alarm went off, pulling her out of her flow. She shook out her right hand with a smile. It had been years since she'd written anything longhand and she couldn't wait to start writing on a computer.

She pulled her phone from the pocket of her sweatpants and shot a text to Caitlin.

ALISSA: ***I think I'm going to be here for a while.***

* * *

Dane ran his hands through his hair, then fixed it as he looked at Alissa's office door. She had been deep in focus all morning, bright optimism in her eyes as she typed. That optimism hadn't faded at all in the entire time she had been working there.

She had closed her door at some point. Maybe she had caught onto him glancing her way more than he wanted to admit. He couldn't help it. Something about her was magnetic. Her optimism was part of it. Even his grumpy self couldn't help but be drawn to it, though he was mostly curious about how she could maintain that energy for so long.

And she was beautiful, and grew more beautiful the longer he was around her. It was safe to think that, but nothing more. She rarely ever wore makeup, but without it, he could see the dusting of freckles across her nose. Her big, wire-rimmed glasses framed her large brown eyes, emphasizing that glow she exhibited all the time.

He ran his hands through his hair again and tried to focus on what was actually important.

Her work continued to be great, but still, he hesitated about her next assignment. He had planned to write an article on the upcoming Cutback Surfing Competition himself since it was a big deal. It happened every year despite the chill in the air and always had a great turnout, at least according to Michael.

If Dane gave her the assignment, Alissa would write a promotional article to get the word out about the event, then a bigger article after she attended. It would require more reporting and research than usual to dig into the history of the event. Whenever he fell into research rabbit holes, hours of his time disappeared into thin air. The more he thought about it—or rather, the more he looked at his ever-growing to do list—the more he was inclined to give Alissa the article.

He got up and walked into the main room of the office.

"Where's Alissa?" Dane asked Josie. "Is she in her office?"

"She went out to lunch." Josie checked the time. "She should be back by now. I'm not sure though."

Dane grumbled. She had the right to go to lunch, of course, but he needed her. He knocked on her door, pausing before opening it. She was gone. Dane let out a heavy breath, studying her office. Even though she hadn't permanently moved all her things to town, she had made herself at home in her office.

There was a fuzzy cardigan across the back of her chair and a few small knickknacks that she had picked up from souvenir shops nearby. It even smelled like her, like summer fruit.

He was about to leave, but the document on her computer screen caught his eye. It wasn't related to the paper, based on the format. It looked like a novel, so he skimmed it. Or rather, he intended to skim it. It drew him in even though he rarely read anything with romance.

The front door to the office opened and Alissa's warm, happy voice floated in. Dane zipped out of her office. Luckily she didn't catch him snooping.

"Hey, Dane!" Alissa said, hanging up her coat next to the door.

"Hello. I have an assignment for you when you're settled in."

"I'm ready right now!" Alissa brightened.

"Let's go to my office."

He let Alissa walk into the office first and came in after her, sitting on his side of the desk. She clicked the end of her pen a few times, sitting on the edge of her seat.

"I'd like you to write two articles about the Cutback Surfing Competition—one article to promote the event, then the other to give a summary of it afterward, so you'll have to go," Dane said. "It's not this Saturday, but the next one."

“A surfing competition?” Alissa scribbled down some notes. “That sounds amazing. What do you want the article to be like?”

“I’ll need you to do some research on the history of the event. It goes back much further than you might think. And capture the energy of the event. Make it appealing to the people of the area, like you do with everything else. It brings in a lot of tourism dollars, especially for this time of year.”

“Got it.” Alissa clicked her pen again and smiled up at him. “I can’t wait.”

CHAPTER TWELVE

Alissa took a big bite of her fish sandwich, humming in pleasure to herself. The fish was fried and the sauce was creamy, but somehow, it managed not to feel too heavy. It made her feel as if it were the middle of the summer, sitting on the beach and enjoying her day. Maybe the freshness of the fish was what made it feel light. She had been in town long enough to know that Braden's fishing company was one of the suppliers for The Crab, so everything was incredibly fresh.

Actually fresh, too, not the "fresh" that she saw at restaurants back in Denver. She wasn't sure how she could go back to eating fish that hadn't been caught that day.

She had tried almost every sandwich at The

Crab, but choosing a favorite was impossible. And it didn't help that there were inventive specials every few days. Some days they were twists on classics like a tuna melt, and other days they invented entirely new sandwiches with other forms of protein or just veggies.

Alissa crunched on a chip and sipped her cider, soaking in the atmosphere. The Crab was always a hub for Blueberry Bay, though the crowd changed depending on the time of day.

The morning was for fishermen coming back in from time on the water. The physical labor made their appetites fierce and they were more than happy to eat at least two sandwiches. Lunch was for people on their lunch break, of course. Blueberry Bay had a few offices for local businesses, and some days it felt like they all went to The Crab. The evenings were the most mixed. Families, students, and other young professionals gathered on the heated patio or inside, enjoying their food and drinks.

Hannah was always behind the counter, serving up food with a smile. She kept Alissa up to date on all the happenings in town, some of which led to articles. Her father Willis sometimes made an appearance too. The gruff man wasn't much for conversation, but he made incredible desserts.

Alissa couldn't wait to dig into one, though she wasn't sure which one to choose. That was a problem for later.

Alissa polished off her sandwich, cleaning her fingers with her napkin before grabbing her pen. She had brought her notebook to work on her book idea. The Crab was the perfect place to do some subtle people-watching for inspiration.

She had her main characters down—the sailor and the siren—and now she was trying to think of the supporting characters. The book was set in an area like this, a small, tight-knit community where everyone knew each other. She tapped her pen on her notebook and looked around the room again.

An elderly couple sat across from a younger couple, smiles on their faces as they chatted. How had they met? Were they related in some way? She couldn't quite tell, but she liked their dynamic. They laughed together, and after some more chatter, someone went to get dessert for the table.

A few ideas clicked in her head. Unlikely friends. Maybe the sailor's best friend was warm and smiley, a contrast to the sailor's. She scribbled down some more ideas until her dinner had settled, then went up to the counter again for dessert.

"What do you recommend?' Alissa asked

Hannah, looking up at the chalkboard menu. "Or I guess the better question is what's left?"

"That is a good question. People have been loving the desserts today." Hannah turned around. "But luckily for you, we have a little bit of everything."

"Ah, now it'll be even harder to decide!" Today's options were key lime pie, mud pie, carrot cake, and gigantic chocolate chip cookies.

"I'll tell you what–I'll put together a little sampler for you so it's easier for you to decide," Hannah said.

"Really? That would be amazing. You're sure, though?"

"I'm very sure." Hannah looked around, a sly smile on her face. "Plus I'm giving myself a little too."

Alissa laughed and Hannah put together a plate with two bite sized portions of each dessert on it. Hannah handed her a fork and dove right into the key lime pie. Alissa followed suit. It was just the right blend of tart and creamy, and the crust contrasted the softness of the filling perfectly.

Then, they moved onto the mud pie. It was another winner–chocolate on chocolate on chocolate with a touch of whipped cream. The carrot cake was moist and the cream cheese frosting was to die for. Topping it off with a bite of the gooey chocolate chip cookie left Alissa farther away from making a decision than ever. They were all delicious.

"Can you pick for me?" Alissa asked. "I think I'll be happy with anything."

"Gotcha! The mud pie is my favorite, so let's go with that." Hannah got Alissa a slice and Alissa paid.

"Thank you!"

Alissa took her pie back to her table and got back to her work. Hannah made a great choice. The pie was decadent but not so heavy that it'd make her want to fall asleep right then and there. She alternated between her work on her novel and questions for the surfing event tomorrow. She didn't notice the restaurant clearing out until Hannah walked past her and turned off the "open" sign.

"Oh, it's so late. I'm sorry—I'll get out of here." Alissa started to clear out, but Hannah waved her off as if to say *don't worry about it.*

"You can hang out. I still have some closing tasks to handle and you look deep in thought." Hannah smiled. "What are you working on?"

"Some work stuff and some fun stuff. Though they're both fun, to be honest." Alissa flipped back a few pages in her notes for her novel. "I'm coming up with questions to ask at the surfing competition tomorrow, and also working on my novel."

"Wow, that's so cool." Hannah grabbed a rag and a bottle of cleaning spray, starting at a table close to Alissa. "What's your book about?"

"A sailor and a siren. At least that's what I'm working with right now." Alissa shrugged, her cheeks warming. On several levels, she knew her writing was good, but talking about her fiction writing when she had put it away for years made her feel exposed.

"I'm sure it'll be great. Your articles are really cool." Hannah wiped down a table and moved onto the next one. "Your life sounds cool, honestly."

Alissa chuckled. "Honestly, it doesn't feel like that sometimes. I'm not as far as I expected to be by now."

"You're doing what you love." Hannah shrugged, moving on to another table. "That counts for something."

"That's true." Alissa studied her notebook, which was quickly running out of blank pages. "Not everyone finds that in life."

"Yeah. I feel lucky that I love working here with my dad." Hannah put down the spray bottle and rag, then went to the cash register. "But sometimes, I kind of wish I could go off and explore the world."

"You always could," Alissa said. "It's not too late."

"You're right." Hannah gave her a wistful smile. "Maybe I will sometime soon."

From the way Hannah said it, that "sometime soon" was far off on the distance. Alissa hoped that Hannah could have some adventures when she felt ready to.

Hannah counted cash at the register for a while and Alissa left her to it. Eventually she went back to tidying up, so Alissa started their conversation again.

"Is this Cutback Surfing Competition a huge deal? It sounds like it's one of the biggest events around here," Alissa said, looking down at her list of questions.

"Oh, for sure." Hannah grinned. "Surfers are a pretty chill bunch."

"And it's been going on for decades, right? I'm still doing some research on it."

"It's been going on for as long as I can remember. And since my dad was a kid at least." Hannah perked up and pulled her phone out of the back pocket of her jeans. "I was just going through some old photos and I think I have one of him at the competition as a little kid."

Hannah swiped through her phone until she

found what she was looking for. She showed Alissa a picture of a very young Willis, squinting into the sun and kneeling next to a surfboard.

"Ah, he was so cute!" Alissa said with a grin, passing the phone back. "Do you think he'd let us use that in the article?"

"I can ask." Hannah tucked her phone back into her pocket. "But yeah, it should be amazing. People come from all over and they're a lot of fun."

"I can't wait to meet people. I never knew anything about surfing up here until I came, so maybe I'll meet someone who's in the same boat." Alissa made a note to seek out a person who came from the farthest spot and interview them.

"You'll love it. Tons of interesting people."

"I'm really excited." Alissa starred a few of the questions she'd written down.

"Make sure to swing by our booth! We're going to have a ton of surf themed specials."

"I definitely will."

Alissa gathered her things and said goodbye to Hannah, energy fizzing through her veins. Hannah was right—she was lucky to have found what she loved and even luckier that she got to do it every day. Plus, her work for *The Outlet* had only boosted her creative energy for her novel.

She hoped she could fall asleep tonight. Tomorrow was going to be great.

Caitlin inhaled the clean, ocean air and let it out in a gust. She had finally made it to Whale Harbor. The town was so small that she had to go from Denver to New York to a smaller local airport. It had been a long time since she'd traveled period, much less in several planes.

Or maybe it felt like a long trip because she had left in the day and arrived in the dark. She walked out of the airport toward the taxi stand, which was one of the few lit up areas around. Back home, it would have been the peak of the dinner rush, but here, everything looked like it was already closing up to go to sleep.

"Hi," Caitlin said to the older woman at the taxi stand. "I'm looking for a cab into town?"

"Of course, my dear." The woman hopped out of the booth and waved down a man standing outside of his cab, reading a book. "Did you have a nice trip?"

Caitlin blinked, taken aback by the kind question. The woman sounded like a grandmother asking her grandchild about their vacation, not a stranger.

"It was long, but I'm here," Caitlin said.

"Glad to hear it!" The woman stepped back. "Here's your cab—have a nice evening!"

"You too." Caitlin rolled her bag toward the cab, but the cab driver met her halfway.

"Let me help you with that," the man said with a smile, reaching for her bag. Caitlin gave it to him and he put it in the trunk. "Where are you headed?"

"To Literary Stays, please." Caitlin got in the back seat and told him the address.

"That's a nice little spot," the man said, pulling off. The roads were pretty much empty, at least on this side road. "Are you here on vacation?"

"I am, sort of."

She supposed it was a vacation in that she was escaping from her day to day life, but the emotional work she had to do was heavier than that. The way Alissa had described the town made it sound like the perfect place to clear her head away from James and the tension at home. Her daily walks, even in the coldest weather, weren't doing the trick anymore.

And she wanted to see where Alissa wanted to move and talk some sense into her. How had Alissa come here on vacation and immediately set up her life with a job? It was just the impulsive act that she expected from her twin. Alissa had always done things on a whim, often to mixed results. Sometimes it was something minor, like hastily cut bangs, but others were like this—something with the potential to send her life spiraling off in the wrong direction.

Then again, here she was—showing up without telling Alissa she was coming first. If she had told Alissa, they would have fought about it. Caitlin knew her twin well. She had to use a bit of Alissa's style to catch her off guard and get her message across.

Caitlin looked out the window for the rest of the ride, taking in the scenery after the cab driver sensed she was tired and not up for chatting. They drove along a beachside street once they were closer to town, which was beautiful, even in the dark. The few street lamps lit up the tall grasses and sand dunes, and a lighthouse stood tall in the background. Waves crashed against the beach, illuminated by moonlight.

"Here we are," the cab driver said, pulling up to a quaint house near the water. A few lights were on in the windows, but it also looked like it was ready to close up for the night.

"Thank you." Caitlin took her bag from the driver and paid him.

She took another deep breath—the coldness of the air didn't bother her as much since it was so clean. Then, she went up the stairs to the house. Before she even entered, she could see why Alissa would like it. Odes to famous authors were tastefully integrated into the design of the house and in the objects in the front window.

Caitlin knocked on the door and was soon greeted by an elegantly dressed woman with fun, stylish glasses. The woman smiled and opened the door all the way.

"Hello! Welcome! You must be Caitlin," the woman said, extending her hand. "My name is Monica."

"Lovely to meet you." Caitlin shook her hand firmly and stepped all the way inside the house.

It smelled like a library, the scent taking her straight back to childhood when she and Alissa would be holed up there for hours. Caitlin appreciated how the literary theme was noticeable, but tasteful—not too over the top. She saw pictures of the bed and breakfast online, but they hadn't done it justice.

"Let me help you with your bag. Your room is ready upstairs." Monica took Caitlin's bag. "Then I can give you the tour if you're up for it. I'm sure you had a long day of travel."

"It was pretty long but I'd love a tour."

Monica guided her toward a winding staircase and started going up. Some of the art on the walls likely referenced literary works, but they were beyond Caitlin's knowledge. Alissa probably knew.

"What brings you here?" Monica asked. "You look so familiar."

"My twin sister is actually staying here," Caitlin said... right as Alissa stepped into the hallway upstairs.

Alissa looked like she was winding down for the day, dressed in leggings and an oversized sweater. She stopped in her tracks, eyes widening behind her glasses as she stared at Caitlin.

An awkward pause stretched out between them, though Alissa's mouth opened and closed as if she were trying to say something. Finally, Alissa approached Caitlin with her arms open.

"Wow, hi, Caitlin," Alissa finally said, giving her sister a hug. "Welcome to Whale Harbor."

CHAPTER THIRTEEN

"I've just sent you the paper's final layout," Josie called out to Dane from her desk.

"Thanks," Dane replied, opening the email that had just landed in his inbox.

It was only eleven thirty in the morning, but he was on fire, checking off task after task on his to-do list. And the list was long. Every Friday was like this —cranking through everything they had to do to publish the paper on Monday morning. It really made him earn his weekend. Or it would have if he ever took a full day off.

He looked over the paper laid out as it would be printed, ensuring that everything looked just right. One of Alissa's articles was on the front page, and he took a moment to reread it. It was great, as all of her work was. Even the most mundane article about a change in the trash pickup route or new school buses was engaging with her words.

Her article promoting the Cutback Surfing Competition was one of her most well-received pieces. She had captured the excitement of it without having been to it before. Her ability to pull great quotes from people, no matter who they were, was something Dane hadn't seen in a writer in a while. And she found some great photos of locals who had been to the event as children, which added even more flavor to the piece.

Despite having lived there for a short amount of time, she knew what made the town tick. He'd even heard that the expected attendance of the competition was going to be higher than ever this year. Was Alissa's article the cause? He wasn't sure. But if he were in a local's shoes, he would have been enthralled by the idea of it because of her.

The layout looked perfect, so he sent it back to Josie with his approval. Then, he checked that off his to-do list and stood, stretching. When was the last time he'd gotten up and gotten the blood flowing to his limbs?

He walked out into the hallway and peered inside of Alissa's office. Instead of her usual sunny optimism, she had faint dark circles underneath her eyes and her shoulders were hunched. Dane rapped on the door as to not startle her.

"Hey, you're welcome to take a long lunch today." He checked his watch. "It's around that time."

"Oh, it is." Alissa checked the time too. "Thanks—it gives me time to get lunch with my sister."

Her usual upbeat tone was notably flat.

"I never knew your sister lived in town." He leaned against her door frame, tucking his hands into the pockets of his dress pants.

"She doesn't." Alissa squeezed the bridge of her nose under her glasses. "She showed up unannounced."

"You don't seem too excited about that."

Alissa took her glasses off and cleaned them on her big green sweater, a furrow in her brows. The color of the fabric played well against her brown eyes. "I mean, I am. But I'm also not, if that makes sense."

"It kind of does."

"Basically, we don't see eye to eye on a lot of things. We're twins but we're opposites. She owns a restaurant with her husband, has a daughter, and is extremely put together—pantsuits, high heels, all of that. I, on the other hand, up and moved to a town that I was supposed to vacation in for a week or so." She gestured vaguely toward her oversized sweater and wild curls. "Also, I have a wardrobe filled with clothes just like this and I can't walk in high heels to save my life."

"It's a good thing walking in heels isn't a requirement for writing."

"Yeah, I would definitely not be a writer if that were the case." Alissa snorted, putting her glasses back on. "Caitlin thinks that I should settle down and do a 'normal' job instead of trying to become a writer."

Dane ran a hand through his hair, studying her closely. It was so rare to see her in anything but bright spirits. Now her lovely features were drawn in, filled with ambivalence. He could relate. Back when he was in college, people told him it was nuts to go for a career in journalism. Now he was here, the owner of his own publication.

"Your passion for writing is admirable in my opinion. It's worth chasing a passion, even if it's not what everyone else would do," he said. "You've been here for a few weeks and you've already put that passion into every piece you've written. It shows."

Alissa's cheeks colored. "Yeah?"

"Yeah. Josie recognized it first. I was almost too stubborn and blinded to see it too." He paused, but Alissa's open expression put him at ease.

"Why do you think that is?" Alissa asked.

Dane paused again to consider the question.

"Sometimes I get so laser focused that I don't see potential where I should. I just want to see the facts in front of me, if that makes sense," he said.

"It does." Alissa's voice was soft.

"I get so caught up in the business of it. It's all numbers and marketing and advertising revenue," Dane continued. "I forget about how great writing feels and how powerful it can be. It's been a while since I've embraced it instead of treating it like something that brings me joy."

The back of his neck heated at the confession, but he kept his cool. He hadn't been that candid with anyone in a while, especially someone at work. Opening up about his feelings made him feel so exposed, but Alissa was going to treat him with care, not like he was weak. It was a nice change from the cutthroat environments he had been in as an adult. So many people had used his rare moments of vulnerability to their advantage. It had hardened him against people when he didn't need to be, at least not to everyone.

"You could get back to appreciating it the way you used to. If you want, I mean," Alissa finally said.

"Maybe." He cleared his throat and looked down the hallway. Just because he was getting comfortable with Alissa didn't mean he was happy to talk about his feelings at length. "Anyway, are you ready for the surf competition?"

"Absolutely. Are you?"

"Absolutely not." Dane tried to imagine himself standing around on a beach, watching people surf. It was as foreign of an idea as him actually surfing himself, as much as Michael tried to convince him to give it a shot. "It's not my thing."

"How so?"

Dane shrugged. "Just isn't. I don't really do big events. The crowds... things like that."

His excuses were weak and he knew it. But telling her the real answer—that it was an unknown—felt like sharing too much.

"Oh. Well, you can always change your mind and come if you want." Alissa checked her watch again. "Ah, I have to get going. See you after lunch."

"See you."

Dane watched her put on her coat and leave, then decided to go get lunch as well. Despite the chill in the air, he walked all the way to The Crab ten minutes away to give himself time to think.

He wished he could embrace things the way Alissa could. She had jumped head first into all the new quirks and experiences the town had—the way things closed early, long conversations with strangers at the store, seeing the same people walking around town day after day. All of these things were the opposite of city living, but she had taken them on just fine.

Maybe she was right. With her on board writing such good articles, he could afford to get back in touch with the part of him that craved new experiences. It was going to be a big change, but it was going to be worth it.

"Hey, Alissa," Caitlin said as her sister walked through the door of Literary Stays. She closed her book and put it aside.

Caitlin had been enjoying the front library, as Monica had called it. It was more of a sitting room than a library, a place where people could gather and chat rather than curl up and read. But it was closer to the dining room than the main library and Caitlin wanted to greet Alissa at the door, so she had stayed there for most of the morning.

She had intended to spend some time thinking about what she'd come here to get through, but she ended up wrapped up in a book. That was the point of the room, she supposed. It was impossible not to want to curl up with a book in there.

"Hey! I'm not late for lunch, am I?" Alissa pulled off her hat, making her wild spiral curls even crazier.

"No, you're right on time." Caitlin resisted the urge to calm Alissa's hair. "Monica said it should be ready right about now."

The two sisters walked to the dining room, which was adjacent to the front library. The smells of rich lentil, kale, and sausage stew made Caitlin's stomach growl even though she had been more than sated by the quiche Monica cooked for breakfast.

"Perfect timing!" Monica said as Caitlin and Alissa sat down. "The soup is ready."

Monica served them both, topping off the meal with thick, crusty bread and a winter green salad. Caitlin was immersed in the restaurant world, so having something this delicious and homemade was a treat. The stew warmed her belly from the inside out, and the bread was so perfectly textured that she wanted to meet the baker who made it and ask about their secrets.

"How was your morning?" Alissa asked Caitlin.

"Good. I relaxed and read a book." Caitlin glanced up at Alissa. "How was your morning at work?"

Alissa hesitated, buttering a slice of bread. "It was great. Fridays are usually busy but all of us got a lot done already."

Caitlin nodded. "So you still like it?"

"Yeah, I do. I think Dane is loosening up a little bit and he's really loved everything I've written." Alissa's face was bright with excitement, but then she raised an eyebrow. "Why?"

"I just wanted to make sure that you still liked it because you got the job spontaneously," Caitlin said, dunking her bread into her stew. "Sometimes spontaneous things don't work out."

Not that Caitlin knew firsthand. It had been a while since she had done anything spontaneous, aside from this trip. The last time might have been before Pearl was born and she and James had gone on a weekend vacation to Montreal. That felt like centuries ago, back when they could talk for hours without an awkward gap or a glance at their phones.

When she told James that she was taking this trip

for a few days, he had just said 'okay' and told her that he could take time off to stay at home with Pearl and had everything at the restaurant under control. No 'I'll miss yous' or even questions about why she wanted to randomly make a trip out to Rhode Island in the middle of winter.

Her heart sank into her stomach just thinking about it. She assumed he'd at least show *some* concern or at least curiosity. He still loved her, yes, but was he still in love with her?

"I think this is working out pretty well. I was such a mess back in Denver." Alissa laughed, the brightness coming back into her eyes. "Then I stumbled on a job that just happened to be a great fit in a great town. I didn't know I needed something like this. I really love my work and my creative energy is back. I'm even working on a novel I put aside years ago. I lucked out."

It was good luck. But that was the crux of it—luck. So much about Alissa's life was chaotic and subject to the whims of whatever was around her. What if she hadn't heard about this job at *The Outlet*? What if her boss wasn't a fan of her writing style? What if this bed and breakfast wasn't as nice as it appeared to be on the outside? So many factors could have gone wrong.

But everything had come together and Alissa was happier than Caitlin had seen her in ages.

Caitlin took a spoonful of stew and ate it, trying to suppress the burning jealousy in her chest. Even though Alissa's life was chaotic, she loved it. And having everything in order wasn't a guaranteed way to stay happy, that was for sure. The only thing that Caitlin felt was perfect was how it all looked on the outside.

"I'm super excited about my next assignment," Alissa said, putting down her bread. "Did you know that surfing is pretty big around here?"

"No, I didn't."

"It is, and there's a big competition tomorrow. I already interviewed some people in my first article about it, which was more to build excitement for the event. It was great. There are a lot of old timer surfers who used to use these boards that were ridiculously heavy compared to the modern ones." Alissa's words came out in a rush, like she couldn't wait for Caitlin to hear them. "They had so many great stories that I'm talking to a few of them tomorrow too. The old boards are going to be on display, kind of like an exhibit alongside the competition. Do you want to come?"

"While you're working?"

“I’ll be observing and talking to people. It’ll be fun.”

Caitlin stirred her stew and thought about it. It was either the competition or she’d be here all day, reading and worrying about what to do with her marriage.

“Sure, I’ll go with you,” Caitlin said.

CHAPTER FOURTEEN

The beach was alive like it was the middle of the summer, not a sunny but chilly day. Surfers with their boards, spectators, and judges milled around, talking excitedly. A row of food booths, including one from The Crab, were on the far side of the event, preparing for lunch time. Vendors were managing crowds of guests alongside them.

Alissa had never seen or felt this level of excitement in Blueberry Bay, and it was contagious. She tried to soak it all in and savor it so she could recapture it when she was writing. It was such a magical feeling --- everyone together, looking forward to the same thing.

"This is such a great turnout!" Alissa said,

tugging her hat down so it covered the tips of her ears.

"Yeah, there are a lot more people than I thought there would be," Caitlin said. She tucked her hands into the pocket of her peacoat. "Where should we go?"

"Hm..." Alissa looked around at all the different groups of people. Most of them were surfers at this hour, dressed in wet suits and stretching out, but there were clusters of spectators gathered on the bleachers, huddled together with warm drinks. She had a wealth of people to talk to. "Let's just take a walkthrough to decide."

They were on the side of the event closest to the parking lot, so they walked straight through. Alissa said hello to a few people she knew, including Michael, the owner of Tidal Wave Coffee in his wet suit. Several people were hanging on his word, laughing along with him when he told a joke. He was clearly the favorite—none of the other surfers had as many people around him as he did.

Alissa hadn't had the chance to talk to him about his surfing career yet, but she told Dane she wanted to write a piece on him someday. She just knew he had some interesting stories in him, ones that no one in town knew.

Alissa's head spun with possibilities for her article on the event and she pulled out her notepad, trying to walk and take notes at the same time. Did she want to talk to a young family first, or some people who were examining the surfboards with an expert's eye? Or did she want to talk to some vendors to see how the event was in comparison to last year? Or maybe a surfer who could tell her about how the waves were? The hardest part of this assignment was going to be narrowing it all down.

Even Caitlin had lightened up, taking in all of the excitement as they reached the end of the competition space. It didn't take away Alissa's worries about her, though. When she first arrived, Alissa assumed her visit would be filled with lectures about her decisions. And yes, Caitlin was more than happy to talk to her about that. But sadness lingered around her twin everywhere she went and she hadn't opened up about it.

Later. Alissa had to give her sister time or she'd retreat into herself again. There had to be more to this visit than Caitlin was saying.

"I think we should find a place to watch the competition since it's going to start soon," Alissa said, her eyes scanning the bleachers.

But then she spotted a shock of bright auburn

hair under a dark blue cap, the man's tall frame familiar. Was that Dane? She took a few steps forward and confirmed it. He didn't look like he did at the office at all, though he fit in with what everyone else was wearing. Instead of his usual tailored shirt, slacks, and pea coat, he was wearing a big jacket, black joggers, surfer sunglasses that he likely picked up from a vendor, and a knit cap with a surf brand logo on it.

Alissa held in a laugh. It was like he'd tried to be his own opposite for a day.

"Stay here, I'll be right back," Alissa said to Caitlin, squeezing her shoulder and approaching Dane. He was so focused on the activity that he didn't notice her approaching. "You said you weren't going to come."

"Well, I changed my mind. I didn't have a lot to do this morning and I figured I'd stop by." He shifted his weight between his feet and took off his hat, running his fingers through his hair. It stuck up in five different directions "If the paper is covering it, it would make sense for me to come. Purely business."

The corner of Alissa's mouth quirked up in a smile. "So if it's just business and it makes sense for you to be here, what's with the disguise?"

"Fine, you're right." Dane chuckled, cupping the

back of his neck, like he was trying to hide how red it had gotten. "Is my disguise that bad?"

"It's not bad at all."

In fact, she liked it. The only other time she had seen him in vaguely casual clothes was at The Crab, and even that had been much dressier than how the locals dressed. Seeing him in joggers and a big jacket, his usually tidy auburn hair windswept, made her heart skip a beat.

"Do you want to sit with me and Caitlin?" Alissa asked, gesturing toward the bleachers. "We were just about to sit down."

Dane paused for a moment, then said, "Sure."

Alissa guided Dane over to where Caitlin was waiting, looking out onto the ocean.

"Caitlin, this is my boss, Dane. Dane, this is my sister, Caitlin," Alissa said.

"Nice to meet you," Dane said, giving Caitlin a firm handshake.

"Nice to meet you as well. Want to grab a seat?" Caitlin asked.

"Sure, go ahead," Dane said, stepping aside so the sisters could go up the bleachers first.

As they walked up, Caitlin shot Alissa a look and a secretive smile. Alissa knew that look well from every other time that Caitlin suspected something was going on between her sister and a man. It was ridiculous, so Alissa ignored her.

They found a spot on the bleachers with a great view of the ocean, and minutes later, the first heat of the competition started. Alissa was on the edge of her seat, her notepad perched on her lap. The first few surfers, all wearing a different color wetsuit, ran into the water, waiting for waves. Then, they started catching them, some surfers hopping on their boards and gliding along the waves with ease while others struggled.

The look of elation on the surfers' faces when they were successful was infectious. Alissa wondered how that felt, aligning with nature in that way. She wasn't athletic, but she wasn't as uncoordinated as people assumed. Surfing required a whole new level of strength and balance that she knew she didn't have, but everyone had to start somewhere.

"This is convincing me to take surf lessons sometime," Alissa said to Caitlin.

Caitlin laughed, blowing into her gloved hands to warm them up. "Maybe in the summer, I hope?"

"Oh, definitely. I'm not meant for all this cold weather."

. . .

The next few heats passed by with a few surfers going on to the next round. Alissa had a whole page of notes and questions to ask by the time the next round started. What was it like, plunging into that cold water? How did they analyze the waves? How long had they been surfing? Those were just the tip of the iceberg.

Eventually Caitlin stepped away to go to the bathroom during the break between rounds, leaving her and Dane alone.

Dane had been quiet, observing the competition and chiming in from time to time. Now that there was a break, he peered over Alissa's shoulder at her notes.

"Looks like you have a lot to write about," he said.

"Yeah. I have so many questions." Alissa ran her hand down the page, feeling the indentations of where she had pressed down with her pen. "Sorry in advance for all the length you're going to have to cut. "

Dane chuckled. "I'll live. I'm sure that the article is going to be great. I'll give you as many pages as possible."

"Thank you."

Dane tried to smooth his hair again, but the wind

blew it around. His eyes were pensive in the way that Alissa was particularly fond of.

"What is it?" Alissa asked.

"Nothing. Just thinking about being here. Coming here."

"What made you change your mind?"

"Your enthusiasm inspired me to come, if I'm being honest. I'm glad I did," he said. "It's nice to see where you'll take your inspiration from."

Alissa bit her bottom lip to stop herself from grinning. She savored every piece of himself that Dane gave her; she could see it wasn't easy for him.

"I'm glad you came too," she said. "There's so much in this place that has me inspired. The people, the scenery."

"I see."

She hoped he did and would. He deserved to see the magic in the area. She tucked her pen into the spiral binding of her notepad so she wouldn't click the end of it repeatedly. "It's helping me write my novel. I'd love to be a novelist someday."

"I know," Dane said. "I read a little bit on your computer while you were out."

Alissa gasped, her entire body going hot under her jacket. "You what?"

Suddenly, every positive thing she thought about

her draft dried up and blew away. What did he think? What if it changed how he thought about her writing for the paper? Or worse, what if he thought romantic stories were silly? They weren't silly to her at all—love was one of the most important experiences in life and stories about it mattered.

"I know, I'm sorry." Dane held up his hand. "I meant to look at your screen for a second, but then I got sucked into it. I almost always read non-fiction but I thought it was great."

"Oh." Alissa relaxed. "Thank you. I'm glad you liked it. Even if you were snooping a little bit."

Dane's smile, such a rare sight, made Alissa want to smile too. The way he looked at her with warm curiosity was also rare. Usually when she caught him watching her at the office, his gaze wasn't this soft.

"Would you consider going to The Crab with me for dinner sometime?" Dane asked. He paused for a fraction of a second and added, "Just to discuss writing, of course."

Alissa lit up. "Sure, that sounds like a lot of fun."

CHAPTER FIFTEEN

Caitlin never lounged in bed like this back home, sitting in her pajamas well past breakfast time. After the exciting day at the surf competition, both she and Alissa were worn out, so they were taking it easy. So far she had gone downstairs to eat breakfast and lunch, grabbed a book from the library and read it in bed, and even took a short nap.

She sat up and looked out the window at her picturesque view. Her view wasn't of the ocean like Alissa's was, but it was still stunning, showing off the beautiful trees and cliffs beyond that. Something about its purity and emptiness stirred up a melancholy feeling inside of her.

Maybe it wouldn't have felt that way if James were there with her, enjoying the view in silence.

She wished they could somehow renew the romance and passion they once had. It had disappeared so slowly and subtly that she didn't know when it started to fade—a rescheduled date night one week turned into a skipped date night for months. The little notes that they left each other became more and more infrequent. Then the worst of it, the shift in the little things, like kissing and holding hands.

Caitlin sighed and got out of bed. Being in here had a great view, but she was in her head too much.

She went downstairs and found Monica tidying up.

"Hi there," Monica said. "I made some mulled wine not long ago. Would you like some?"

"Sure, that sounds delicious."

Monica left to make the mulled wine and Caitlin went outside onto the porch to take in the view there. Alissa was on the porch bench wrapped in a blanket, a space heater several feet away. Her laptop was resting on a small table next to a steaming mug of mulled wine. Her fingers flew over the keyboard and she didn't even look up at Caitlin until she was right next to her.

"Hey," Alissa said, scooting over to make space for Caitlin on the bench.

"Hey. Hope I'm not interrupting." Caitlin sat down. "Working on your novel?"

"Yeah. My hands need a little break anyway." Alissa made a fist, then opened it several times. "What are you up to?"

"Waiting for some mulled wine. I wanted to check out the view down here."

Alissa picked up her mug of mulled wine and offered it to Caitlin, who refused it.

"Monica is bringing me some, but thank you."

"Okay, but what are you really doing here, Caitlin?' Alissa asked, her voice soft. "Because I know you want to stop me from making rash decisions, but coming all the way here unannounced? That's a little different. Are you okay?"

Caitlin had been mentally preparing for this conversation for a while now. She could tell that Alissa saw what was churning underneath her put together surface, but she wasn't sure how to say it. All of the waiting around made her realize she just had to come out with the truth. Alissa wasn't going to be mean to her.

"No, not really. James and I are growing apart and it's making things hard, especially for Pearl." Caitlin took a blanket off the back of the bench and wrapped it around herself. "She's been acting out in school and I feel like such a terrible mom."

Letting out the admission gave her some release, letting a bit of pressure off the valve.

"You should have told me before." Alissa squeezed Caitlin's hand before tucking it back under the warmth of her blanket.

"It's nothing drastic. We aren't screaming at each other or anything and Pearl still has good grades," Caitlin said. "But there's no passion anymore and I was hoping that coming here would allow me to clear my head. To see things from a fresh perspective."

"This is a good place to think."

"Yeah. I think I still need time to figure it out further, but that's the gist of it."

"Take as much time as you need."

They sat in silence for a few moments, the pressure continuing to leak from inside of Caitlin. Just telling Alissa made her feel this way, and that was the first step she needed to figure herself out. She couldn't think if her thoughts were consumed with how to say it.

Monica came outside with a mug of mulled wine for Caitlin, then disappeared inside again. The wine was just what she needed on a cold day like this—the cloves and cinnamon warmed her up better than a blanket ever could.

Now that her mood had finally shifted, Caitlin wanted to talk about Alissa for a while.

"It was nice meeting Dane yesterday," Caitlin said, a sly grin spreading across her face.

"I'm surprised it took you this long to bring him up." Alissa closed her laptop and picked up her mug of mulled wine.

"Well, he's pretty cute. And he gives you *that look.*"

"What look?"

"The look of someone who's interested in you."

Alissa rolled her eyes. "Remember the part where I told you he was my boss? I can't date my boss."

"Eh, it's a small town. And a very small business. Considering how well you're doing there, you're basically like business partners."

Alissa shook her head and laughed, her curls bouncing. "Okay, maybe. And he did ask me to dinner at The Crab on Monday after work."

"I told you!" Caitlin laughed too, but sobered. "Wait, you're not going there directly after, are you? You're coming home first?"

Alissa shrugged. "I wasn't planning to. It's a ten

minute walk from the office to The Crab so I thought we'd go together."

"Nope, that won't do." Caitlin wrapped her finger around one of Alissa's spiral curls. "You need to get dolled up before, and I'm going to help you. You can't go on a date in your combat boots, sorry."

Alissa snorted. "Fine, it couldn't hurt. But don't go too far—Dane said it was just to talk about writing and he's still my boss."

"I know, I know," Caitlin said. "We can still have a lot of fun with a little makeover."

"Hey, Ross," Dane called when he noticed his friend looking around Joe's, Blueberry Bay's only bar.

It was a far cry from the cocktail bars where they sometimes met up after work back in Manhattan, but it was nice. It had a long, wooden bar along one side and small tables throughout, just big enough for groups of three. Everything had a tinge of age and wear to it, but it was pristine underneath the scuffs.

Joe, the owner and namesake, was always behind the bar, serving up a menu of mostly beer and basic cocktails. He had been a fisherman when he was younger, so much of the clientele was the same.

Dane had sometimes gone at off hours if he wanted a change of pace or if he wanted a drink and The Crab was too busy.

"Hey!" Ross smiled and crossed the bar. "How are you?"

"Not bad. How are you?"

"Not bad either." Ross slid onto the barstool next to Dane. "Sorry I'm a little late. I couldn't find this place."

Joe's didn't have an online presence whatsoever, and it blended in with the rest of the town so well that it was easy to walk past it—a true hole in the wall. Music was always playing, but it wasn't so loud as to draw attention from the sidewalk. Dane didn't blame Ross for missing it at all.

"No worries."

"So this is your local drink spot?" Ross looked around. He looked almost as out of place as Dane had when he first arrived. Much like Dane did most of the time, Ross dressed well in a blue and green striped sweater, a pea coat, and dark jeans.

Today Dane had dressed down a little in a flannel shirt, faded jeans, and some older boots that he didn't wear often. After the surfing competition yesterday, he felt more comfortable going out in more casual clothes. He hadn't realized how dressing up was a shield for him in some ways, making him a little less approachable. He didn't plan to wear jeans to work, but he could loosen up outside of the office.

"Not my main place, but I've been here a few times. I'd take you to The Crab, which is my main spot, but I'm going there tomorrow. As much as I love it, I still feel a little weird being a regular at places. They know my name, what I usually like, and even what we talked about last."

"Wow. You don't find that back in the city all that often."

"What can I get you fellas to drink?" Joe asked, wiping down the bar in front of them. He studied Ross for a moment, then handed him a paper menu.

"I'll just take whatever IPA you have," Dane said.

"And I'll have..." Ross scanned the list. Joe kept beers from a few local places in rotation, but he rarely ever carried the fancier brands that Ross was used to. "The same, I guess."

Joe nodded and went to the fridge underneath the bar, coming up with two bottles. He placed them in front of each man and popped the lids before going to help someone else.

"What's going on at The Crab tomorrow?" Ross

asked, tentatively sipping his beer. He nodded in surprise when he realized it was good.

"I'm meeting up with one of my writers. Well, my only writer."

"Your writer?" One of Ross's eyebrows lifted.

"Yes, why?" Dane felt his neck heating up, but he hoped that the redness wasn't visible in the low lighting. He was looking forward to dinner with Alissa more than he could ever admit out loud. Just talking about her made his heart clench.

"You got this weird look on your face. What's this writer's deal? You aren't firing him, are you?"

"Her. And no, I'm not firing her."

"So it's a date, then. You can only go red like that if it's a date." Ross's smile grew. "Again, what's the deal?"

Dane picked at the label on his beer bottle. "It's not a date, I swear. We're just meeting up to talk about her writing. And writing in general. She's fantastic—I'll grab you a copy of the paper so you can see her work—and she's very enthusiastic. She reminds me of why I used to love writing. Or the way I used to be when I wrote, I guess."

Ross took another sip of his drink. "So you like her."

Dane shot him a glare. "I do, but not like that. It's not a date."

"You can claim something isn't a date all you want, but I've known you for a long time, Dane."

"Ross."

"Sorry, man." Ross sighed. "I'm glad she's working out. But also, since when did you fall out of love with writing? It didn't sound like it the last time we talked. When was that? A month or two before you left the paper?"

"I guess that feeling snuck up on me." Dane shrugged. "I think I was in such a frenzy trying to keep the paper afloat that I didn't realize how much I'd fallen into a cycle of not truly loving what I was doing. At least I realized it and I'm getting better."

"That's great."

It was. He still had a long way to go in finding that feeling again, but it was starting to heal itself.

"How's life treating you otherwise?" Ross asked. "Are you used to not being able to have anything and everything delivered to you at any time of night?"

Dane snorted. "Yeah, that's one of the biggest adjustments. But it's quiet. The food is great, even though there are fewer options. I'm getting used to feeling like I know every single person. And yesterday I went to a surf competition for the first time and it was a lot of fun, surprisingly."

"A surf competition? Up here?"

"Yeah. Alissa—my writer—is writing a piece on it. I wish you had been there to see it. People came from all over the country, and some from outside it," Dane said. "Everyone was so enthusiastic and excited to be there. It was a good time."

"Huh." Ross studied Dane's face for a few moments. "I never thought you'd be enthusiastic about something like that."

"Enthusiastic is a stretch." Dane was never effusive, but he supposed he was close enough to it for Ross to call him out on it. "But I guess I'm finding a new appreciation for the place."

Talking about it out loud to Ross made the realization even starker. He didn't feel like he was one hundred percent local yet, but he was starting to see the things that had chafed against him when he first moved there in a new light—how small talk was always a little drawn out, how people took their time, how they took an interest in everyone as if they were their friend.

Ross caught Dane up on everything happening back in New York over another round of drinks, and eventually, they walked through town to *The*

Outlet's offices. After showing Ross around, Dane gave him a copy of the paper and walked him back to his car, promising he'd be in touch more often.

As Dane went back to his car and drove home, he tried to think of ways he could use this newfound revelation about himself to make something great. He had some vague ideas, pieces of dreams he'd long since left behind. Maybe Alissa was just the person to talk to about them at dinner.

CHAPTER SIXTEEN

Dane's coffee was out to get him.

He gasped, catching his coffee cup just before it spilled all over his keyboard. A few drops splashed onto it, but nothing that would cause damage. He sighed, putting it on the far side of his desk where it was within reach, but if he somehow knocked it over, it wouldn't soak his computer.

Today he had dropped his latte moments after picking it up at Tidal Wave Coffee, so the barista had to make a new one for him. Then, on the way out, he nearly tripped and sent it flying. When he got back to the office, Alissa said hello to him as he took a sip and he'd choked on it trying to respond.

And then there were the work-related mishaps. He spent a half hour copyediting the wrong file, deleted an article he was mostly done with (though thankfully he had a backup), and forgot to attach documents on three separate emails.

As much as he didn't want to admit it, all of his clumsiness and carelessness was because of nerves. He was having dinner with Alissa at The Crab and he didn't know how it was going to go. They talked and had connected over writing, but what if it was awkward or changed things between them?

He stood up and stretched, trying to shake the nerves. It wasn't a date, as he'd told Ross. It was just talking over dinner. Alissa had a lot of interesting things to say, and he wanted to hear them. That was it.

So why were his hands sweating?

He ran his hands through his hair and sat back down, getting ready to focus again. It was five-thirty and he wanted to finish his work and go home to freshen up before he met Alissa at The Crab. He made it through his final tasks by six and gathered his things.

"Wow, you made it through the day without burning down the whole office," Josie teased.

The back of Dane's neck heated up, but he feigned innocence. "What do you mean?"

Josie raised an eyebrow at him. "Dane."

He shrugged his coat on. "Okay, you're right. I've been a bit of a klutz today. It's Monday."

"True, true." Josie glanced to the corner of her computer screen. "And you're heading out early on top of that."

"Yeah, I'm just going home to freshen up." He tucked his hand into his pocket and started to meander toward the door.

"Freshen up and go where?" Josie sat forward on the edge of her seat, her smile broadening.

Dane knew Josie wasn't going to let this go, so he said, "I'm going out for dinner with Alissa, but not like a date. We're just talking about writing. It's no big deal."

He expected her to continue with her good-natured ribbing, but to his surprise, Josie's expression sobered. "Ah."

"What is it?"

"It's just that Alissa is special. It's not every day that someone comes into your life who can change your perspective," Josie said.

Josie was right. Not only had his actual work gotten easier since Alissa was such a fantastic writer, but it hadn't felt like drudgery like before. Finding news wasn't like pulling teeth anymore, and the small town things that had bothered him before, like everyone knowing who you were, weren't as bothersome either. She had even changed his mind and convinced him to step out of his comfort zone.

Dane could only shrug in response—putting those feelings into words wasn't easy.

"I'm just saying that Alissa has inspired you to loosen up a bit," Josie continued. When she saw Dane open his mouth to respond, she held up a finger. "Even if you're trying to pretend she hasn't, I can tell she's made an impact on you. I've seen your change up close and personal, Dane."

Dane checked the time, his stomach doing flips inside of him. "I have to get going. I'll see you tomorrow."

"See you. Have a great night."

Alissa left work a little early, her stomach fluttering the entire commute back to Literary Stays. So many unknowns were in front of her this evening—Caitlin's makeover and her dinner with Dane— and she couldn't wait to see how they panned out.

She went upstairs to her room and found Caitlin inside, standing next to the bed with a pile of dresses stacked up on it. Her desk was equally covered in makeup and accessories, a pile of shoes on the floor. Most of these clothes were Caitlin's.

"Um... hi?" Alissa said, stopping in the doorway.

"Hi!" Caitlin brightened up more than she had most of the trip. "I'm glad you're back. I think I know what direction I'm going to take your makeover. I even did some shopping. There are so many cute little boutiques around here."

"A whole makeover?" Alissa put her canvas tote bag down. "I thought you were just going to help me get dressed up."

"Same difference." Caitlin waved her hand as if to dismiss Alissa.

"You really don't have to go through all this trouble." Alissa picked up a dress. "Wait, you bought this for me?"

"If you don't like it, I'll take it. A perk of being a twin—what fits me, fits you." Caitlin plucked the dress from her hands and held it up to Alissa. "Same with makeup. I didn't see any in the bathroom. Did you bring any?"

"I don't really wear it most days." Alissa shrugged. "But seriously, you don't have to do all this. I'll put on a little makeup and a dress and it'll be fine."

Caitlin sighed and rested a hand on her hip. "No offense, but you look like Skeeter from *The Help*."

Alissa laughed. "How is that an offense? Emma Stone is beautiful."

"She is!" Caitlin took Alissa's hand and pulled her toward the bathroom. "But Dane is gorgeous and this nerdy, slightly rumpled newspaper girl vibe isn't going to work. Put your best foot forward."

Alissa shrugged and let Caitlin steer her into the bathroom. A line of fancy skincare products that weren't there before sat next to the sink, along with palettes of makeup.

"Let's start with skincare. Use this one first," Caitlin said, handing Alissa a sleek pink tube. "It's a cleanser."

Alissa did as she said, relief washing over her as she cleaned her face. Caitlin had always been better with this kind of thing, and Alissa wanted to look good for Dane. He always looked good, like he put time into his appearance every day without going too overboard. Like his outfit today— one of his tailored shirts and a green cardigan that was the same shade as his eyes. Alissa wouldn't have minded if he wore the same thing to the date. Or dinner. Whatever this was.

"Wow, my skin is so soft," Alissa said after she

finished with the cleanser and its accompanying lotion. "You use this every day?"

"Yup." Caitlin took a step back and studied her twin's face. "Let's pick out an outfit before we do your makeup."

They went into Alissa's room again, looking at the pile of clothes on the bed. Alissa's wardrobe was mostly neutrals and earth tones—they were easy to match when she was in a rush to get out the door. But the clothes on the bed were much more Caitlin, all bright, coordinating colors.

"I think a dress, tights, and boots would be perfect," Caitlin said. "Dressy, but casual enough to blend in at The Crab."

"I can't remember the last time I wore a dress." Alissa picked up a hot pink dress. "This is a little much. People could use me as a marker if they were lost at sea."

"It's not *that* bright." Caitlin took the dress from Alissa and put it aside. "How about a deep red dress?"

"Sure, that's not too big of a leap." Alissa picked up a long-sleeved, garnet red dress that cinched at the waist and flowed to a few inches above her knee. And more importantly, it looked comfortable. "It's pretty."

"Try it on."

Alissa took it to the bathroom and undressed, pulling the dress on. It fit perfectly and suited her well. It didn't feel like she was dressing up as Caitlin or dressing up like someone else.

"I love it," Alissa said, stepping out of the bathroom.

"It looks great!" Caitlin clasped her hands together. "Dane will love it. Let's do your makeup and hair."

Alissa's heart fluttered at even hearing Dane's name. Caitlin sat her down at the desk in the corner and adjusted the lights so she could see Alissa's face. Alissa let Caitlin take over with her typical take-charge attitude.

"What if I'm reading this wrong?" Alissa asked as Caitlin tapped some tinted moisturizer on her face. "What if he literally wants to talk about writing and nothing else? What if it's not even close to a date?"

"I've seen him look at you. I'm pretty sure he asked you on a date while convincing himself that he didn't." Caitlin snorted and picked up some blush, swirling a brush into it.

"I hope so."

Alissa had thought about dating back in Denver,

but not in a serious way. The dating scene was overwhelming and she couldn't find anyone she clicked with. But Dane felt different. Ever since they first met, he had sparked her curiosity. His grumpy exterior, intense focus, and devotion blended together to form one interesting package. But he'd started to show what was underneath, little by little —the encouraging, earnest man who showed up to the surf competition and watched it with a writer's eye.

"Okay, your hair," Caitlin said. Alissa hadn't realized she was done with her makeup. "I'm not sure of what to do."

"Well..." Alissa played with her curls. "Something not this."

"Of course." Caitlin played with Alissa's hair. "I know just what to do."

With some creative uses of pins and hair spray, Caitlin transformed Alissa's hair into a fun updo that suited Alissa well.

"Voila!" Caitlin guided Alissa in front of the bathroom mirror.

Alissa could hardly believe it was her. Most days, she rolled out of bed and wore a comfortable outfit she'd worn a million times, but now she was polished and not overdone. The dress flattered her figure and the color complemented her brown hair and eyes. But at the same time, she looked like herself.

"Thank you, Caitlin. I look amazing."

Caitlin beamed. "No problem. I know you'll wow him."

CHAPTER SEVENTEEN

Dane needed to kill time.

He had taken his time going from the office back to his house, taking the roundabout way that gave him a scenic view. But now he was home and had about forty minutes until he had to leave.

He kicked off his shoes at the door and wandered deeper into his small home. When the realtor had shown it to him, she had apologized for how small it was. He had almost laughed in response. This was the largest place he'd ever lived in as an adult and he had a washer, dryer, and a dishwasher, three appliances that were luxuries in individual apartments back in New York. It was more than enough for him.

He went back to his bathroom and washed his

face, then changed into something more comfortable and casual. It took almost no time at all, to his chagrin, and he wasn't going to kill time trying on a bunch of different outfits. He looked fine. And after a spritz of cologne, he smelled great.

Was cologne going too far? It wasn't unusual for him to wear it to the office, but putting it on specifically because he was going out with Alissa felt odd.

He shook that thought off. This wasn't a date. It was a dinner to discuss writing. His anxiety levels were entirely disproportionate to the stakes of the date. He just wanted to get to know her more. And he was her boss.

With a sigh, he went into his living room to kill even more time and to keep his mind off of what was to come.

He wasn't much for decorating, so most of his décor was his bookshelves, stuffed to the brim. He had been meaning to get another one but he hadn't gotten around to it yet. Instead of starting something new, he plucked an old favorite off of his shelf—a biography of Nikola Tesla.

The biography was expertly done, bringing the scientist's story to life in a way that never got old. But his eyes kept drifting down the page without absorbing any words. He kept up the ruse until he could finally leave for the date. No, the casual dinner.

•

He showed up to The Crab first, feeling so fidgety that he stuffed his hands into his pockets despite the warmth in the restaurant. The Crab was busy for a Monday night, but there were plenty of tables available for him and Alissa. He wasn't sure whether to sit and wait for her to arrive at a table, or if he should linger around the door to greet her there.

Willis and Hannah were working, as always, tidying up and preparing sandwiches. Dane came regularly, so they said hello.

"Hey, Dane," Willis said, nodding at Dane as he sliced a sandwich in half. "Need some help?"

"Not yet. I'm just waiting for someone." He stepped to the side so he wasn't in the doorway.

"Oh, cool. A friend?" Hannah straightened up some salt and pepper shakers along the narrow bar along the wall.

"Alissa."

"Oh." Hannah swept her ponytail over her shoulder, curiosity in her eyes. Willis, though gruff, was undeniably curious too. "Well, I hope you guys have fun."

"Thank you." Dane's neck was burning hot, so he took his coat off, hanging it on the back of a chair.

He sat down, trying not to jiggle his leg or stare at his phone. Luckily, the door opened moments later and Alissa walked in. His stomach fluttered when she looked his way and smiled. She looked beautiful —she was wearing a little makeup, emphasizing the natural loveliness that he saw every day, and wore a deep red dress that he'd never seen her wear before.

He couldn't form words as she approached, but when she said hello, he regained his ability to talk.

"You look great," he said, standing up. 'Great' didn't cover how he felt, but his brain was still coming back online from seeing her for the first time.

"Thank you." Alissa's cheeks went pink. "You look great too. Have you ordered yet?"

"I haven't."

They left their coats at the table and went to look at the menu. He rarely ever stood right next to Alissa, especially not close enough to take in how nice she smelled.

Focus, he thought to himself, looking up at the menu.

Alissa ordered a fish sandwich and their hand-cut fries, and Dane got the same. Dane couldn't help but notice the curiosity and delight in Hannah's eyes as she took their order, but he chose to not show that he saw it. He was hyperaware of everything and everyone as they walked back to their table. It felt like every pair of eyes was on them, even though logically, Dane knew they weren't. The table wasn't big, so when they sat, their long legs brushed against each other. Alissa slid backward, a shy laugh escaping her mouth.

"And two hard ciders on the house," Hannah said, appearing behind Dane and putting them on the table. "They have a hint of grapefruit and lime in them."

"Thanks, Hannah!" Alissa said with a smile. Once Hannah was gone, Alissa lifted her bottle. "To writing?"

"Sure, to writing." Dane tapped his bottle against hers and took a sip. He usually wasn't a cider person, but this one wasn't too sweet. The acid of the citrus cut through the sugar, making it go down smooth. "Speaking of writing, I've looked at what you wrote on the surf event. It's great."

"That's great to hear! I had a lot of fun watching. I've never seen anything like it. I'm glad you made it too." She blushed, looking down at the table.

"I'm glad I did too." Dane liked the shy, but excited look on Alissa's face. It was the same one she wore when he complimented her work, particularly something she had put a lot of time into. "You really captured all of the facets of it—the surfing, of course, the spectators, and vendors, all of that."

The light in Alissa's eyes was contagious. "You didn't think my article was too long because of it?"

"It was a little long, but all of it was so interesting that I kept most of it," he said. "I might make it a two part piece."

Alissa beamed. "That's so exciting. I can't wait to tell Caitlin."

Dane hadn't gotten the chance to speak to Caitlin one-on-one, but the differences between her and Alissa were obvious. Caitlin was much more prim and collected than Alissa, and she had a certain sadness in her eyes as she looked out into the water.

"How is Caitlin?" Dane asked. "How has her visit been?"

"It's been better than I thought. She gave me the talk about my career and life choices early on, but she mostly came to escape." Alissa's eyes softened. "Her life back home is stressful and she needed some time to figure things out."

"This place is really rejuvenating for people," Dane said.

"It is. I hope she gets unstuck." Alissa bit her bottom lip, concern filling her eyes.

"Here we go," Hannah said, appearing with two red baskets filled to the brim with their dinners. "Two fish sandwiches."

"Thanks!" Alissa pulled a napkin from the holder and put it in her lap. "This is one of my favorites."

"They're all good." Dane followed her lead. The sandwiches at The Crab rivaled any of the ones from the best sandwich shops back in New York City. Everything was fresh, especially the fish, and they put inventive spins on old classics.

They enjoyed their food in silence. Dane savored Alissa's presence as well. Sitting across from her here outside of the office made him realize just how natural being around her felt. She exuded positivity and openness, even when she wasn't talking. He felt like he belonged when he was with her.

"How's your novel going?" he asked, popping a fry into his mouth.

"Good! I've been working on it in the mornings. The sunrises from my room at Literary Stays are unreal," Alissa said with a dreamy sigh. "It's just flowing, you know?"

He knew the feeling well. Or at least he used to.

Getting into the zone and having the words fly made time go by in an instant.

"That's great." He took a sip of his cider then swirled the drink around in its glass bottle. "How does Caitlin feel about that?"

"I think she's more okay with it than she is with me up and moving to a place where I thought I was going to visit for a little while." Alissa chuckled. "But that's to be expected. In case you didn't notice, we're twins but we're opposites."

"I did notice." Even the way they carried themselves was different.

"I understand her in some ways. Stability is comforting. But at the same time, I'd prefer to chase my dreams and my passions and maybe fall down than stand still. Like when I wanted a job with *Epic*, I read every single back issue I could get my hands on. It was an obsession but it helped when I finally landed an interview."

The corner of Dane's mouth quirked up in a smile. He could easily see Alissa doing something like that, tearing through issue after issue, one heel on her chair and her knee resting on her chin as he sometimes found her in her office.

"And even though that didn't work out, I came here on almost a whim and it's been the best thing that's happened to me in a while." Alissa tucked one of the curls that had come undone from her hairstyle back into place. "It was impractical and maybe a little crazy, but I'd prefer that to leaning into practicality and getting stuck."

"Do you feel that's why your sister is stuck? She's too practical?"

"I think that's part of it." Alissa contemplated that. "When we were in our early twenties, I always thought I was so behind in comparison to her. She had a nice boyfriend, got married, had a baby, started a business... and those are fulfilling to her but she clung to them."

"To the point where she's not letting herself take a risk."

"Right. Sorry, I've been going on and on about my life," Alissa said with an embarrassed smile.

"I like to listen to you. We usually just talk about work." Dane reminded himself that was what this was supposed to be about, but now they were talking about her dreams and taking risks. "You're a passionate person so I'm not surprised you're open to talking about it."

Alissa cleaned her fingers and tucked the used napkin next to her red basket. "What about you, then? You took a big risk starting this paper out here when you were used to living in New York City. How do you feel about it now that the paper has been going well?"

Dane gathered his thoughts so he could answer with the same thoughtfulness and consideration that Alissa had.

"It's been better. I still care to the point of working myself a little too hard, I think. But being out here has been better for me than I thought. My passion for writing had faded with the breakneck speed of everything in New York. It's hard to really get into something when it's going to be swept off your desk minutes later."

"I get that."

"And my old workplace wasn't ideal." Dane let out a humorless laugh. "I was rushing around, trying my best to make everything fit together and my old boss didn't care."

"People misused semi-colons one too many times?" Alissa teased.

Dane raised an eyebrow at her, though his gaze was still light. "They did. I take my semi-colons very seriously."

They both laughed.

"But anyway, it was rough for me there. I was putting in all of my blood, sweat, and tears, and I wasn't getting much in return. Finally I just snapped one day and walked out," he said. "I was preparing to become the co-owner of the newspaper and was mad at myself for blowing up that opportunity. But it's turned out okay. I'm starting to see the potential of a newspaper out here now that we have a great writer on board."

Dane wasn't one for giving a ton of compliments —in fact, past writers he worked with often said he was ridiculously hard to please—but giving them to Alissa felt natural. Plus, he enjoyed her smile after, which grew despite her trying to keep calm. Her giddiness was always contagious.

"So newspapers have always been your passion?" Alissa asked.

Dane picked at the label on his cider bottle. "I'm not sure if they've always been a passion, but they've been a part of my life. I was the head of my paper back in high school and college and I was always writing. When I was a kid, I was obsessed with Superman because well, he was Superman and he was a journalist."

"So stories are the overarching theme there."

"Exactly."

Alissa polished off her sandwich right as Dane did. "That was so good, but the pie of the day has been calling my name ever since I saw it on the menu. Want to split dessert?"

"Sure, key lime pie sounds great. I'll get it for us." Dane got up, taking their empty baskets and stacking them next to the trash, and bought them the key lime pie. He pointedly ignored the big grin on Hannah's face when he said he needed one slice, but two forks. She threw in extra ciders on the house as well.

"I don't know how Willis makes pies this good every single time," Alissa said after taking the first bite. "And I didn't used to be a pie person."

Dane took a bite from the other side of the pie. It was perfect—the creamy-citrusy taste combined with the perfectly crumbly crust was just the right ending to their meal. They tore through the pie and switched to enjoying their ciders.

"If you could do anything for work, what would you do?" Alissa asked.

"Anything?" Dane took a moment to think. "I used to want to start a magazine. I know it doesn't sound all that different than starting a newspaper, but it is. More long form content, less aggressive deadlines."

"Wow, that's a great idea!" Alissa said.

"You think so?" His eyes widened.

"Of course. I mean, you're already getting a

sense of what people around here like. Having a magazine gives you an opportunity to take a deeper dive," Alissa said.

Dane nodded slowly. "Like with your piece on the surf competition—it could have been a great cover story. You could have had all the space you needed."

"That sounds amazing." Alissa beamed. "Why not do it? People in town already trust *The Outlet*. I'm sure they'd love to read longer pieces about hidden gems around here. Or about things they thought they knew, but from a different perspective."

He liked that—seeing what was here from a different perspective. It was exactly what Alissa had done. She had seen all of the people, those who Dane hadn't thought to talk to, and pulled out fascinating stories. So much was there, just waiting for them to uncover it together.

"I think it could work. With your help and vision, of course," Dane said.

"I'd love that."

They talked about the possibilities for a magazine about the region, tossing ideas back and forth almost as fast as they could come up with them. Eventually, The Crab started to close, so they went outside, their breath fogging in the cold.

Dane suddenly became hyperaware of where his hands were and where Alissa was standing, much closer to him than she would have in any other circumstance. Before he could question his instincts, he leaned in and pressed a soft kiss to Alissa's lips. It had been a long time since he'd kissed someone, and he'd never felt this swell of joy and contentment while doing so—like everything was exactly as it should have been.

When they broke apart, they rested their foreheads against each other for a moment, trying to gather themselves. Dane had seen Alissa smile a lot, but never quite like this. He wanted to see that smile again and again.

Alissa couldn't remember the last time she had smiled this hard, or the last time she'd had such a perfect kiss, if ever. Dane's grass green eyes were bright, a touch of a smile on his lips too. It was a look he rarely gave anyone, so it felt special—a hint of who he was underneath his serious expression, the version of himself he kept hidden away.

"What are you thinking about?" Dane asked, tucking a loose curl behind her ear.

"I was just thinking about how I never thought I'd ever see you smile when we first met." Alissa laughed, running her fingers along the soft threads of his sweater underneath his coat. "You were so uptight!"

Dane chuckled, then smiled, one side of his mouth creeping up higher than the other. "Me? Uptight? I have no idea what made you form that impression."

Alissa snorted and Dane broke out into laughter again.

"I can see why we butted heads," Alissa said.

"Clearly we worked it out." He slid his hand down her arm, lacing his fingers in hers. "Want to take a walk?"

"I'd love that."

Alissa savored the warmth of his hand as they started toward the boardwalk, which was lit up by both the moon and lamps. A few other people were out too, some couples like them and some groups of friends. Alissa was glad Dane had suggested they walk. She didn't want this date to end just yet.

The moon gleamed over the water and clouds drifted across the sky, creating a dreamy scene that only added to the fluttery lightness in her chest. It was like she was in a movie.

Dane had the pensive look on his face that Alissa was very used to. She let him gather his thoughts instead of jumping in and distracting him.

"It's funny that you say I'm uptight. If you asked teenaged me if I was like that, he would have laughed," Dane said.

"Seriously?" Alissa tried to imagine him as a teenager. "I would have imagined you as the brooding, angsty type, locked in his room with a bunch of books and journals."

"I *was* usually in my room with books and journals and loud music, but I was pretty carefree, at least in comparison to now." He squeezed her hand, almost unconsciously. "My dad was the rigid and serious one, so I didn't want to be like that. I always wished he'd loosen up and have more fun like other dads."

Alissa nodded. Her parents weren't like that at all, but she understood how stifling that could be.

"I never saw myself becoming like him," Dane continued. "But then I woke up one day and realized that all the work and my ambitions had turned me into him. The weight of all those responsibilities was heavier than I thought."

"I bet it was stressful. There were probably a

billion more moving parts to a large paper like that, and you had to be responsible for all of them."

Alissa couldn't imagine working on something that big. She'd miss the closeness that came with working on such a small publication. *Epic* had felt huge too and she had been so disconnected from her coworkers that getting to know them was an extra job in itself.

"It was." Dane gently pulled Alissa to the side so a biker could pass. "No wonder I was so cranky all the time. Once I was staying late and groaned just like my dad did whenever he was dealing with something frustrating. It scared the crap out of me."

"I bet. As much as we say we won't turn into our parents, we always do in some ways," Alissa said.

"True. He's a good man, but even now that he's retired, he's stuck in his routine." Dane nudged Alissa. "I probably would have gone down that road too if you hadn't come along and pulled the rug out from under me. It's hard to be crabby and rigid when you're so optimistic and passionate."

Alissa blushed, her smile turning shy. "Really?"

"Yes."

Despite the warmth filling her chest, a cold breeze made her shiver. Dane slid his arm around her shoulders without skipping a beat. He was warm and smelled clean, like fresh laundry. It was such a comfortable, natural gesture, and that realization made her heart race. How had they gone from butting heads to feeling exactly right?

Alissa slipped closer to him, setting aside her fears for now. She didn't want to ruin this moment with doubts and anxiety about things that might never come to pass.

They walked along the boardwalk, chatting about things they saw when the moment felt right and embracing the comfortable silences that came in between.

Soon the chill got to be too much, even with Dane's warmth cocooning Alissa, they headed back toward the parking lot near The Crab. Once the cars were in sight, their steps slowed, like they were trying to drag out the last moments of this date as long as they could.

Alissa glanced up at Dane, wondering if their post-dinner walk and their reluctance to end the date meant that he wanted a second one. She definitely did, but she didn't want to get too far ahead of herself.

"This is me," Alissa said, stopping next to her sedan. "I had a nice time."

"I did too." Dane slid his hand down her arm and intertwined his fingers in hers.

He leaned in and kissed her again. The second kiss was even better than the last, soft and sweet. Alissa had already grown addicted to how nice he smelled up close, and knew she'd probably sniff her coat to see if his cologne lingered on hers when she got home.

She could have stayed here in the parking lot, safe in his arms for hours, but it was late and they had work to do tomorrow. He squeezed her hand and stepped back.

"See you tomorrow," he said, barely containing his grin.

"See you."

Alissa didn't stop smiling the entire drive home.

CHAPTER EIGHTEEN

Alissa hummed to herself as she added a little extra cream into her coffee. She already knew she'd need a second cup at some point in the day once her happy buzz faded. Dane had occupied her thoughts all night, so she didn't sleep much. All of their ideas for the magazine and talk about chasing dreams had her invigorated and ready to work on her novel despite the early hour.

She flitted around the kitchen, debating whether to grab a bite to eat yet, when Monica came downstairs.

"Good morning!" Monica said. "You beat me down here."

"I did. I was just staring at the ceiling, waiting for an appropriate hour to get up, so I figured I'd just hop up and get the day started." Alissa sipped her coffee. "I'm too amped up."

"Is it because of your date?"

"Yeah." Alissa grinned thinking about how easy it all felt, like she and Dane had clicked in a way they never had before. He had looked so handsome sitting across from her, his spring green eyes intent on hers as he listened. "It was perfect. We ended up talking until The Crab closed and we kissed."

"That's so exciting!" Monica pulled a big purple mug from the cabinet. "Are you going out again?"

"I'm not sure." Alissa bit her bottom lip. "I'm not sure if it's a good idea to be catching feelings right now. Plus he's my boss, and even if this is a small town, that's kind of unusual."

"It seems like you've made a lot of changes lately but they've all been for the better. Falling for someone seems like just another good thing. And honestly, it's not that weird to date your boss around here. You have a common passion that most people don't have around here."

"True!" Alissa cupped her mug with both hands, savoring the warmth. "It's all so exciting, and so much all at once. Moving here, my job, Dane's ideas, my book."

Alissa had gotten up early before work most days

to work on it, and she was excited to take her coffee upstairs to dive back into it again. She was three-fourths of the way through and loving it. Every time she looked out onto the ocean, new scenes popped into her head.

The sunrise was the most inspirational part of the day to her. It was as if the sailor and the siren were out there somewhere and she was just writing down how their relationship was unfolding.

"How's your book going?" Monica opened the fridge and came out with cream.

"It's great. I've already sent my old college professor the first half and she really liked it. She thinks she has a publisher in mind and knows some people there, so my manuscript will go to the top of the list once it's done."

"Wow, that's incredible!" Monica put a touch of cream in her coffee and stirred it. "When do you think you'll be done with the book?"

"Soon, if I keep going at this rate. I already know how the story is going to end, so I just have to stick the landing, so to speak." Alissa topped off her coffee, then added more cream.

"We'll have to do something for your book's release!" Monica pushed her glasses up on her nose, looking past Alissa's head. "A signing and an event. The library would be so perfect for that! And if it came out in the spring or summer, we could do something on the lawn. I've been meaning to do more events like that."

"Whoa, slow down." Alissa laughed. "I have to actually finish it. And while my professor thought I had a good shot, nothing's been guaranteed yet."

"I've read your writing for *The Outlet* and what you've told me of the story sounds amazing," Monica said. "I just know you'll be published. And I'm going to buy copies for each library in here and for the library in town."

Alissa's worries faded—Monica's belief in her bolstered her confidence. Between her novel, the new magazine, and her feelings for Dane, a whole new world of opportunities was opening up for her. She had no idea where they were going to take her, but she was excited to find out.

* * *

Dane leaned back in his chair, putting a leg up on his desk the way he did when he was alone in the office. His phone burned a hole in his pocket, waiting to be looked at. Had Alissa texted him? It was only eight in the morning and they had ended their date less than twelve hours before.

He caved to his instincts and pulled his phone from his pocket. No texts, but he wasn't disappointed. He opened a new one to Alissa, his thumbs hovering over the screen. She was going to be there in an hour, maybe less. Was texting overkill?

He really liked her. It had been ages since he'd been on a date where he went home feeling like he was walking on air. And he knew Alissa had a good time too, so he texted her. Why bother trying to hide the fact that you were into someone?

DANE: Hey, I had a nice time. Thank you for coming to dinner.

Response bubbles popped up immediately.

ALISSA: Thanks for inviting me. I had a great time too. It really inspired me, and I've been writing this morning.

He smiled.

DANE: ***That's great.***

Reply bubbles popped up, then disappeared several times before another message came through.

ALISSA: ***Can I ask you something?***

Dane sent back a *yes*, and her next reply came in soon after.

ALISSA: Yesterday was a date, right?

He chuckled to himself. Who had he been kidding? It had been a date since the moment he asked. Why had he thought that he wasn't falling for her?

DANE: Yes, it was absolutely a date. And I'd like to go on more of them.

She sent back a smiley face emoji, its cheeks pink.

ALISSA: ***I would too. I have to get going. See you in a bit.***

He put his phone down and turned back to his computer. Their conversation last night had inspired him too. Alissa had gotten to the root of a lot of the things he had been thinking about: his passion, finding it again, getting the most about what the area had to offer. The magazine was going to be the perfect addition to the area. It was the exact kind of writing he loved reading and writing.

He grabbed a pad of paper and a pen since writing his ideas out by hand always produced better ideas. After writing *magazine ideas* at the top, he got to work, his hand moving as fast as it could as ideas poured out of his head.

Eventually his computer pinged with a new

message, distracting him from his work. The email wasn't important, but Alvin's unread message caught his attention. Before he could second-guess himself, he finally opened it.

Hi Dane,

I know the last time we spoke, things weren't going well between us. That's kind of an understatement, isn't it?

To cut to the chase, though, you were right about everything you told me the day you quit. Without you, things have hit bumpy waters.

Dane blinked. He'd guessed that this could be what Alvin's email was about, but now that he was seeing it with his own eyes, he couldn't believe it. Alvin hardly ever admitted he was wrong like this. Instead of feeling a flush of satisfaction, he just felt his mood dip. He read on.

I know that you've left to start a paper up in Rhode Island. I'm sure you'll have the vision to take you wherever you want to go. But if you decide not to pursue that, I'd love to have you come back. We can discuss co-ownership of the paper too.

Give me a call whenever you get this. You know my cell number.

-Alvin

Dane sat back in his seat, slightly numb. Did he regret not opening this sooner? It would have given him the confidence boost that he needed before Alissa came along. But now he was confident on his own and feeling sad for Alvin. Dane almost laughed. If his past self saw him now, feeling bad for Alvin despite the way things had fallen apart, he wouldn't have believed it. He wouldn't have believed that his future self was beginning to like this place, either.

He dialed up Alvin, waiting for him to answer with a knot in his chest. Alvin picked up at the last ring.

"Dane! I've been waiting for your call," Alvin said.

"Yeah, I'm sorry for the delay. Things have been busy." Dane raked a hand through his hair.

"I bet." Alvin cleared his throat. "Listen, did you give any thought to what I talked about in my email?"

"I have. And as much as I appreciate it, I think I'm meant to be here," Dane said.

Alvin didn't speak for several beats.

"Ah." Dane could feel Alvin's disappointment despite not seeing his face. "That's not what I was hoping to hear."

"I know. But it's the truth. Things are working out here. Running smoothly."

The other man chuckled. "I need a little bit of that magic back here. I'm sorry for not recognizing how much you did around here to keep things afloat. I've been... well, not drowning, but barely treading water. I know I used to be able to run this place, but now I feel lost."

Alvin's voice was so vulnerable that Dane almost didn't believe it was him. But it was.

Dane bit the inside of his cheek. "You can make the paper the way it was before on your own. More organized. Less about clicks and more about putting out good work. Your writing is what inspired me to apply to the newspaper all those years ago."

"Yeah?"

"Yeah. It's just a matter of recapturing the memories of how you felt before."

"Easier said than done," he huffed.

"It's possible. I found it out here." Dane

shrugged even though Alvin couldn't see him. "I'm sure you can too. Without dropping everything and moving to a tiny town most people haven't heard of, of course. Maybe a vacation will help."

Alvin paused. "I hope so. I've been meaning to get away. Thanks, Dane. I've got to go. I hope we can stay in touch."

"I hope so too," Dane said, meaning every word.

He hung up, contentment filling his chest. Even though he'd left in an angry rush, he believed in Alvin. If he could find himself again, anyone could.

* * *

"How about here?" Alissa asked Caitlin, nodding at Sally's Soup, a soup and salad lunch place that she sometimes went to when she wanted something light, but warming.

"Sure, this works."

They crossed the street and went inside, joining the small lunch rush. Caitlin had met Alissa outside of *The Outlet*'s offices so they could walk to lunch together. Unlike the first time Alissa had lunch with Caitlin during the workday, Alissa was in a better mood and she had been ever since her date with Dane on Monday.

Alissa glanced over at her twin, who was looking up at the board with the soups of the day on it. Caitlin still hadn't lost that emptiness in her eyes, even in a moment as small as this.

They each ordered something different so they could try each other's soup—Alissa went with pumpkin sage and Caitlin went with chicken and rice. The restaurant was small and busy, but they found a table near the front window.

They dug into their soups and tasted each other's. Both were delicious, just the right lunch for a cold day, but Alissa was glad she had gone with the pumpkin sage.

"What have you been up to?" Alissa asked.

"Not much." Caitlin shrugged, pushing a chunk of chicken around in her soup. But then, she brightened. "Pearl's teacher sent me this adorable video of her. I have to show you."

Caitlin dug her phone out of her purse and scrolled around, then propped her phone up so they could both see it. Alissa's heart grew as she watched Pearl sing along to a song, a big grin on her face. Her hair was up in lopsided pigtails that made her look even cuter.

"That's so cute. Can you send it to me?" Alissa asked.

"Yeah." Caitlin took her phone back and sent it over. "Pearl's teacher said she's been doing a lot better lately. She's reading a grade level ahead. And that little girl next to her in the pink sweater is her best friend now."

Caitlin watched the video again, a mixture of emotions on her face. But it was clear that she missed Pearl more than anything else. But that left her husband, James, behind and their relationship was the reason why she'd come here.

Alissa waited for Caitlin to put away her phone and go back to her food before she spoke again.

"You've talked a lot about Pearl, but how are things with James?" Alissa asked.

The sparkle in Caitlin's eyes faded. "I don't really want to talk about him right now."

"I know it's hard, but didn't it feel better to open up last time?" Alissa nudged Caitlin with her foot.

Caitlin sighed, tearing off a piece of baguette that had come with her soup. "I guess you're right."

Still, Caitlin took a few moments to gather herself. Alissa waited, not wanting to interrupt whatever chain of thought she was forming.

"I talked to him again the other night," Caitlin said. "And I don't think we got anywhere. I have no idea how we could possibly get to that better place where we used to be. If we were even there in the first place. Now I'm not so sure."

Alissa thought back to James and Caitlin's wedding. They had looked so in love and so happy. And when Pearl came along, they were elated.

"You guys have had great times together," Alissa said. "Anybody could see that you guys were in love with each other."

Caitlin took a deep breath and let it out. "That's good to know. But it feels different now. Like the distance between us, like we're two individuals living in a house, parenting our daughter instead of a married couple. But I bring this up to him and he doesn't see it at all. He says he feels the same way as he always has. That's the last thing I wanted to hear. How can I fix a problem if he doesn't see one? I feel so alone in this."

Caitlin took another deep breath and shakily let it out, as if she were trying to temper her emotions. Alissa reached across the table and gave her twin's forearm a squeeze. Her heart went out to Caitlin, more than it ever had.

"I don't have the answers, and even if I did, I can't tell you what to do. But no matter what you decide, I'll support you."

Caitlin finally smiled, her eyes soft. "Thanks, Lissa."

Alissa smiled back. Even though they had their differences growing up and hadn't always been close because of their approaches to life. But as they got older, the more those differences faded to the background. They were sisters at the end of the day, and all of these changes in both of their lives had brought them closer than ever. Deep down, they wanted the same things—happiness and fulfillment—and that allowed them to see eye to eye more.

It filled Alissa's chest with a different kind of lightness, one that she hadn't expected.

"I'm glad you came, Caitlin," Alissa said.

"I'm glad I did too."

They went back to eating, chatting about how incredible all the food tasted. Caitlin's palate was much more sophisticated than Alissa's, so Alissa was glad that she loved the food around here just as much as she loved the food back home.

"How have things been at work since your date with Dane?" Caitlin asked.

"Really good," Alissa said, a smile touching her lips at just the thought of Dane. "I was a little worried it was going to be awkward, but it hasn't been at all."

"Yeah? When are you guys going out again?" Caitlin leaned forward to sip her iced tea out of her straw.

"I'm not sure. But we both want to." Alissa bit her bottom lip, trying to contain her smile. "It was just so nice. So easy and right."

A pang of guilt filled Alissa's stomach. They had just been talking about all of Caitlin's relationship problems and now she was gushing about the butterflies in her stomach that came with a new relationship.

But Caitlin's eyes didn't hold a hint of jealousy or displeasure. "That's great! Do you know what you want to do for your next date?"

"I'm not sure what we'll do, but I know it'll be fun." Alissa ate a spoonful of soup as she thought about it. "Maybe we could do something a little offbeat, like surfing lessons or something."

"Surfing?" Caitlin laughed. "I know there was the surfing competition but that water is probably ice cold!"

"It might be refreshing!" Alissa laughed too. "Something different. Something to break Dane out of his shell even more. He's really started to brighten up."

"No more hiding behind surfer sunglasses and

beanies?"

"Definitely not." Alissa paused. "But I'm just worried that he'll close back up again if things go the wrong way. Plus he's my boss, so that throws another wrench into it."

"He seems like a good person, and if he's changed this much in such a short time, I'm sure he'll keep going that direction," Caitlin said, cupping her iced tea glass with both hands.

"I hope so."

Caitlin sipped her tea, gazing down at her mostly empty plate, and Alissa took that moment to study her sister. Years ago, Caitlin would have chastised Alissa for dating her boss, but now there wasn't a hint of judgment in her eyes. Caitlin just wanted her to be happy, just as Alissa wanted Caitlin to be happy.

They finished up their lunch and headed back outside, their moods bright.

"See you back at the B&B?" Caitlin asked.

"Yeah, see you then." Alissa pulled her into a hug, giving her an extra squeeze.

Alissa walked back to her office, a sense of peace coming over her. They were so close to figuring out what made them happy, and once they found it, they were going to be fine.

CHAPTER NINETEEN

Caitlin crossed her arms over her chest to stay warm when a gust of wind came over the ocean. Surfers were out on the water in their wetsuits, either impervious to the cold or great at tolerating it. A few of them laughed as they gathered their boards and ran back into the water, which only heightened her melancholy. Laughter was the last thing on her mind, and there was a lot filling her thoughts.

She needed to figure out when to go home, and as much as she knew she needed to, she couldn't pin down a date. She missed her daughter, and her daughter missed her. Phone calls weren't nearly enough and she didn't want Pearl to feel like she had been abandoned after Caitlin left so abruptly.

But the thought of talking to James about their

marriage when so much was still in the air made her chest tight. Being away had given her some rest, but it hadn't given her the exact kind of clarity she craved.

Her phone buzzed in her pocket and she checked it. It was James.

"Wow, weird timing," she murmured to herself, even as her heart pounded. She didn't want to leave him waiting, so she answered. "Hello?"

"Hi, Caitlin," James said. "How are you?"

"I'm okay." Hearing his voice made her heart squeeze. "How are you?"

"Fine."

The silence that stretched between them made Caitlin realize how reflexively she had answered. She had always said she was fine, that everything was great. That was fine with strangers, but James was her husband. Telling him everything was fine even when it wasn't might have been part of the reason why she was in this mess anyway.

"Actually, I'm not fine," Caitlin admitted. "I'm not sure how I am and I don't know when I'm going to come home."

Tears welled up in Caitlin's eyes in an instant and spilled over when she heard James let out a breath through his nose.

"Caitlin... you don't know when you're going to come home yet?" he asked.

"No. I know I should—I miss Pearl and know you need me. But I don't feel ready to come back without answers to why I came out here in the first place." Caitlin took a few deep breaths to get a handle on herself. Her tears chilled her face when the wind hit her skin, so she wiped her face with her knit gloves.

James paused. "Why did you leave in the first place? I thought you were just visiting Alissa."

"I just feel like our relationship is so stagnant and I can't stand it. It's like we're strangers when we didn't used to be that way."

"Ah." Caitlin knew him so well that she could imagine him raking a hand over his face. "I see that, but things at the restaurant aren't going to get any less crazy and we can't work through things if you aren't home."

Caitlin wandered along the beach, pulling up her collar against the wind. "I know. I just needed some space. It's been bothering me for so long and I wasn't able to clear my head with all of the stuff going on at home."

Caitlin heard Pearl's small voice in the background and her heart lurched.

"Pearl is here," James said. "Do you want to talk to her?"

"Yes, I'd love to."

James passed the phone to Pearl.

"Mommy?" Pearl asked.

"Hi, sweetheart," Caitlin said, her voice coming out choked. "How are you?"

"Good! I learned about swamps in school today," she said. "And about crocodiles, which aren't the same as alligators."

"Yeah?" Caitlin clenched her fist in her pocket to keep her emotions in check. "What else did you learn?"

Pearl told her all about what she had been learning in school for the past few days. Caitlin's watery smile grew. How was Pearl growing up so fast? She was missing her, as much as she knew coming here and figuring out her marriage was going to be good for Pearl in the long run.

Eventually Pearl handed the phone back to James.

"Okay, we've got to get going since she has ballet soon," James said. "Just let me know when you're coming back, okay?"

"I will."

Caitlin hung up and put her phone back into her pocket, a few more tears falling down her cheeks.

Alissa curled her socked feet underneath her, turning up her music since she was alone. The office was dark and quiet with just her in it. Everyone else had gone home a few hours ago. While she loved having everyone else there, there was something special and fun about being by herself—her writing flowed even faster than before, her fingers flying over the keyboard.

She dug her hand into a big bag of peanut M&Ms that she kept in her desk, popping them into her mouth. They were far from a nutritious dinner, but she was too in the zone to stop for anything else. She was on the last chapter in her novel and knew exactly what was going to happen. The words spilled out of her exactly as she wanted them and she typed *the end* with a flourish.

"Yes!" She pumped her fist into the air. "Finished!"

She threw back more peanut M&Ms and realized she needed a drink. The fridge in the kitchen nook always had seltzers, so she padded across the space to grab one. She came back and put her feet up on her desk, rereading what she had just written. It was a fantastic ending, if she could pat herself on the back for a moment. It captured the themes of the book and called back to the beginning that made the entire book come full circle.

It wasn't perfect, but she was incredibly proud of what she had done.

The front door creaked open and Alissa jumped. She whipped her head around, her hand to her chest. It was just Dane. Her heart went from pounding to fluttering. He had changed out of the dress pants and tailored shirt and into a thick cable knit sweater, nice jeans, and boots.

"You startled me," Alissa said with a laugh. "What are you doing here so late?"

"I could say the same thing to you. I was just doing well with my work and I wanted to keep going after I had dinner." Dane shrugged off his jacket and hung it up. "What are you doing here so late?"

"Same here." Alissa held up the bag of peanut M&Ms. "And you're a much more responsible adult for going to get dinner. I've been eating M&Ms."

Dane smiled, taking some. "It's an appetizer."

"I like the way you think."

"What were you working on?" Dane asked, going for more M&Ms. "Your book?"

Alissa grinned. It must have been written all over her face. Or all over her whole body, since she was almost vibrating with excitement. "Yup! I finished!"

"Congrats! I think this moment calls for a toast." Dane glanced at her seltzer and disappeared around the corner. He came back with a can of seltzer for himself. "To finishing your book."

They tapped their cans against each other and took sips. After splitting more M&Ms, Dane spoke.

"You inspired me," he said.

"I did?" Alissa asked. "In what way?"

"The way you dove into writing your novel and doing this job made me want to dive into my ideas." He leaned against the door frame to her office. "I haven't felt this invigorated by my ideas in a long time."

"I'm glad to hear it."

Dane shifted his weight between his feet, picking at the tab on his seltzer with his index finger.

"Once your book is a big bestseller, you won't have to live here anymore and work at some itty-bitty newspaper," he said.

"What do you mean?" Alissa raised an eyebrow, a smile in her eyes. "I want to help you create the magazine we were talking about. I'm not going anywhere."

"Really?"

"Of course!" Alissa put her seltzer down. "I think the two of us can tap into the soul of the area and bring people what they want. Or what they didn't know what they wanted."

Dane smiled, running both hands through his hair. "I think we can too. Our differences can definitely be an asset here if we believe in the same goal."

"Exactly." Alissa stood, her can in her hands. "Maybe we can continue that in the future. Inspiring and helping one another. Trying to boost each other's creativity."

"I'd like that," Dane said softly. He took Alissa's hand and pulled her closer. "I think we could make a great team."

He pressed a kiss to Alissa's lips, sending tingles radiating all over her body, then pulled her into a hug. His warmth and the campfire scent of his cologne made her feel safe and protected, like everything was going to be okay.

* * *

"Ready to head out?" Alissa asked Dane, pulling on her coat.

"Yeah." Dane checked his computer one more time before standing up and stretching. "I skipped breakfast this morning, so I'm more than ready to eat."

"You, skipping breakfast?" Alissa grinned. "I wouldn't have guessed."

Dane nudged her as he passed, a teasing brightness in his eyes. His breakfast was almost always a latte from Tidal Wave Coffee, and he always talked about how hungry he was around lunch time because of it.

Dane put on his coat as well and they stepped outside of the office. The air was brisk, but not as bitterly cold as it had been in the past weeks. Alissa loved the way Dane's cheeks got a rosy flush to them after he was in the cold for more than a moment. They had been going out to lunch every day, or at least eating together in the office, and they had gone to dinner a few times too.

Their lunches were a bright spot in her day—fun and casual.

"So, where to?" Dane asked, tucking his hands into his pockets. "Want to walk or drive?"

"Hm, driving might be faster but it's a lovely

day." Alissa looked up at the clear, blue sky, then back at Dane. "I'd prefer walking. We can pass by a few different options and see what we want."

"Then let's walk."

"I hope the boss doesn't mind if our lunch runs a little long," Alissa said with a grin.

"I don't think he'll mind all that much." Dane grinned back, taking her hand in his.

Alissa savored the warmth of his skin as they headed toward town on foot. It was such a small point of contact, but it made Alissa's whole heart light up.

"Okay, first option," Dane said, pausing in front of Sally's Soup. "Soup?"

"Caitlin and I went here not long ago." Alissa scanned the chalkboard sign outside that listed the specials. "Though the soups of the day sound really interesting. I've never had a Thai-inspired shrimp soup before."

"Ah, they don't have the chicken noodle today," Dane said. "Can we keep looking?"

"Sure."

They kept walking, passing by a few shops before Alissa spoke.

"Wait, do you always order the chicken noodle

soup at Sally's? Even with all the different kinds of soups she offers?" Alissa asked.

"Yeah, pretty much."

Alissa snorted so hard that she had to stop. "You cannot be serious. She has a billion different soups!"

"A billion's a stretch." Dane squeezed her hand and tugged her along.

"Okay, fine, but still—there's so much out there but you're sticking to *chicken noodle?* I only eat that if I'm sick. I mean it's good, but still." Alissa shook her head.

"Exactly, it's good." The corner of Dane's mouth quirked up. "Classics are classic for a reason."

"But the same old thing again and again is boring."

"Not if it's delicious," Dane said. "And I've been adventurous in the past. I just like knowing that lunch will be satisfying."

"Yeah? What kinds of foods have you tried?" Alissa glanced at the sign for a Mexican place they had tried a day or two ago for dinner.

"Oh, as much as I could back in New York. I could travel around the world without leaving the city. One month I was ambitious and tried to have some food from at least two countries on every continent."

"Wow. I take back everything I thought about you not trying new things. That's really cool," Alissa said. "I tried to go to as many different kinds of places as I could, but I really loved Ethiopian food the most."

"Ethiopian food is great. Especially with a little *tej* to drink," Dane said. They both spotted the sign for The Crab off in the distance. "But it's hard to beat the fresh fish and the restaurants around here."

"Definitely. I've never had anything like it." The breeze chilled Alissa, and as if he read her mind, Dane put his arm around her shoulders. "I never would have expected the food here to be on par with what I had back in Denver. This town has been filled with surprises, but in a good way."

Dane let out a quiet sound to acknowledge that he'd heard her, but didn't respond right away.

"Yeah, me either. I thought that because everything here closes ridiculously early that it was all low quality. Though now that I've said that, it sounds silly."

"No, I get it. I chose to come here because I knew it would be quiet." They stopped at an intersection.

"I knew it would be quiet too, but I wasn't ready for just how silent." Dane ran his hand up and down Alissa's arm.

"I felt the same way!" Alissa said. "I woke up once because it was so quiet."

"Wow. I listen to white noise at night and it's helped." Dane guided them to the side so they wouldn't walk into a pole. "But aside from that, the peace has been really helpful. Even more than I thought it would be."

"This whole town has been filled with surprises. I really like it here."

"I do too now that I've gotten used to its quirks."

"I'll definitely miss it when I go back to Denver. Or if I go back. I'm not sure." Alissa's brows furrowed. She had always assumed that she'd go back to Denver—she still had her apartment there—but she hadn't spoken about leaving to anyone.

"Mm," was Dane's only verbal response, but Alissa felt his body stiffen.

The casual warmth and camaraderie that they'd had dried up, and Alissa's stomach sank. The shift in the vibe threw her decision into high relief. What was she going to do at this crossroads? She had always been a free spirit, flitting from place to place without forming too many attachments. That was why she had come to this town in the first place—a whim, more or less.

But this town was different. There were things

here that she wanted to keep. The quiet, kind people, the delicious food, the beautiful scenery, and of course, Dane and her job. She had never felt this at peace before.

Maybe it was time to be like Caitlin in some ways, to lay down roots somewhere and not go wherever the wind blew her. Commitment didn't have to be scary like she thought it was. Caitlin might have committed too deep too soon with James, but not all commitment was the same.

Sometimes it meant staying in one place and knowing what worked for you. And sometimes, it was the thing that kept you from missing out instead of the other way around.

Alissa bit her lip. If she went back to Denver, what would she miss out on?

"Do you just want to go to The Crab?" Alissa asked as they approached it.

"Sure, that sounds good," Dane said, his tone still a little stiff.

Alissa brushed it off and put on a smile. She wanted to enjoy this lunch with Dane—she could think about her future a little later.

CHAPTER TWENTY

"Your regular latte?" the barista at Tidal Wave Coffee asked Dane the moment he walked in.

"Yes, thank you." Dane nodded in appreciation and went over to the far side of the bar, leaning against the wall. The stack of copies of *The Outlet* was very low, just as he wanted it to be. Paper sales had been steadily climbing.

"We've been selling out of *The Outlet* lately," the barista said as she prepared a double shot of espresso. "People have really been loving it."

"That's great to hear." He thumbed through the latest issue even though he'd read the paper several times over at this point.

"The article on the surf competition was cool. I wanted to go but I was here. There's always next year, I guess." The barista chuckled and steamed some milk, finishing up Dane's latte. "Enjoy!"

"Thanks," Dane said, lifting his cup and taking a sip.

As always, it was smooth, creamy and perfect. He thought he was addicted to caffeine back in New York, but the lattes here were bringing his love for coffee to a new level.

He went onto the outdoor patio and made a beeline toward a table near a heated lamp, the cold wind cutting across his cheek. Once he sat, he pulled out his phone to look at his to-do list for the day. A lot of his list was made up of things to do for *The Outlet*, of course, but the magazine idea was there too. And along with the magazine came thoughts of Alissa.

Was he ready to jump into a big project and possibly a relationship with someone who had such a different view on life? Like he'd said the night before, their differences could be an asset and he believed that Alissa had changed his mindset and view on life to be more optimistic. She'd brought the area to life for him. But it was still a big leap. All of his feelings were so new and he didn't know how he was going to feel months from now.

He checked his email and marked the ones that

weren't important as read and answered a few that could easily be taken care of right away.

"Hey there," Michael said, approaching Dane's table. "Working on a Sunday morning?"

"Yeah. Can't quite help it," Dane said, looking up. As always, Michael was dressed casually in a way that oozed cool and casual, even though the weather was cold. "The paper is always being written or edited or printed, so there's always something on my plate."

"Very true. Must be fast paced." Michael pulled out the chair across from Dane and sat with his coffee. Instead of a to-go cup, he had his in a huge ceramic mug with the Tidal Wave Coffee logo on it. "But it's a great paper even with the fast turnaround times. I loved the article on the surf competition."

"Congrats on the win, by the way," Dane said.

"Thank you." Michael smiled. "I talked to a lot of my surf buddies and they really loved it. They said the writing was great and captured things about the surfing world that they hadn't even thought of. That's a big feat considering how into the sport some of them are."

Pride radiated through his chest. "That's great. Alissa's great at capturing the nuances of situations like that. She's got an eye for it."

"I hope she sticks around," Michael said, watching Dane over the rim of his coffee as he took a sip.

Michael's look was anything but subtle—it was a mild warning. Did everyone know that he and Alissa had gone on a date? He didn't doubt that at all. News traveled quickly and they had gone to The Crab, which was one of the town's social hubs. If Willis and Hannah talked to other business owners in town, it was only a matter of time before Michael found out.

Dane wasn't surprised at how protective Michael seemed to be either. Alissa's enthusiasm won over almost everyone she met, even the grumpiest like him.

"I do too," Dane said. "I really like her and want her to stay."

Tension fell from Michael's shoulders. "Good."

"And I think she will. We're working on an idea for a magazine—longer form content about the area, finding stories that need more research, things like that." Dane sipped his drink. "Alissa has a lot of ideas for it and she's really excited to get started. That's a big part of my to-do list today. We want to get the plan down for the kinds of articles we want to publish, then see about how to actually pull it off."

"That's a fantastic idea," Michael said. "You should go for it."

"I agree!" the barista said from across the patio as she gathered up some mugs left on the bus station.

The three of them laughed. Dane was reasonably confident in his ideas, but hearing from locals, including one who was very influential, made him even more so. The small town community that he had chafed against when he first arrived was now a warm comfort. He hadn't expected that, but he appreciated it nonetheless.

Alissa sighed, digging through her desk drawers for her emergency stash of peanut M&Ms. She'd had to replace them after hanging out with Dane in the office after hours. They had sat next to each other, eating the candy and talking through ideas. She had gotten so animated that she nearly knocked over her can of seltzer all over her keyboard.

Looking at the candy now reminded her of Dane, making her heart flutter. Whenever he crossed her thoughts, her attention drifted away from whatever she was doing. She was falling for him, hard. Had she ever met a man who challenged her and kept her on her toes, but in the best way? Or a man who was so handsome that looking at him filled her with butterflies every time? She wanted to throw her arms around him in a big hug and take in the scent of his cologne. She wanted to thread her fingers in his and walk along the beach, talking. She wanted more dinners at The Crab, splitting dessert and staying there until it closed.

Alissa snorted, throwing back some M&Ms and chewing. She seriously had it bad.

She looked back at her computer, trying to focus on the article she was supposed to be working on. But she had her personal email pulled up too and her eyes drifted to that. She had edited her manuscript and sent it off to her professor a little while ago. Now all she had to do was wait to hear back from her regarding whether any publishing companies were interested.

That was much easier said than done. Nervous, excited thoughts of possibly finding a publisher rushed through her head in the spare moments when she wasn't thinking about Dane or the magazine they wanted to start. Seeing her name in print at *Epic* and now at *The Outlet* was great, but having something so solid and so permanent like a book with her name on it was still a dream of hers. She closed her eyes, trying to imagine what it would feel like holding it in her hands. That was so far away, but thinking of it boosted her mood. Truth be told, it boosted her impatience too.

Alissa crossed her fingers and toes, hoping that when she refreshed the page, an email would be there. But there wasn't one.

She sighed and got back to work, slowly making her way through her article. Even though she was excited by it, her thoughts kept drifting to Dane yet again. She heard him talking on the phone, his deep voice low and confident. When she got up to go to the bathroom, she passed by his office. He gave her a small smile as she passed that made her heart somersault in her chest.

She came back to her desk right as her phone started to ring. She wasn't expecting a call from anyone, so she answered with a question in her voice.

"Hello?"

"Hi, Alissa! Sorry to call from my office phone, but my cell phone is across my office," Alissa's professor, Dr. Cane, said.

"Oh! Dr. Cane!" Alissa plopped down into her seat. "It's nice to hear from you."

"I have some great news," Dr. Cane said. "I received an answer from one of the small publishers I spoke to, Seashore Press. They love your book and think it'll be a perfect fit for their catalog."

"What?" Alissa's knees went weak even though she was sitting down.

"They want to work with you!" Dr. Cane said. "Congrats!"

"Oh my goodness." Alissa pressed her hand to her forehead. "I'm so... I don't even know how to put this into words. I'm so excited. So grateful. I'm so glad I was sitting down!"

Dr. Cane laughed. "They're a great publisher. Small, but that means that everyone is dedicated to each and every book they publish. One of my dearest friends has a few books with them and only has great things to say."

"A small press is absolutely perfect." She wasn't looking for big accolades or fame—she wanted what she had here at *The Outlet*: a fulfilling experience, even if her reach wasn't big. Publishing this book was going to be just the same.

"I'll email you with more details and connect you with your editor," Dr. Cane said. "I've got to get going, unfortunately, but we'll talk soon!"

"Thanks!"

Alissa hung up and held in a shriek of

excitement. Instead, she darted into the hall and into Dane's doorway, startling him.

"Dane, my book got picked up by a publisher!" Alissa blurted.

"Really? That's incredible, Alissa!" Dane stood up and crossed his office. "Congrats."

He pulled her into a hug, and Alissa squeezed him tight.

"Thank you." Alissa let him go, but he kept his hands on her waist. "I had to try so hard not to scream. My hands are still shaking."

She held her trembling hand in between them, and they both laughed.

"What's the publisher? Do you know when your book will come out or anything like that?" Dane asked, still holding onto her.

"It's a small press, Seashore Press. My professor said they had a great reputation and her friend who had a few books with them really loved it," Alissa said. "I don't know anything else yet but my professor is going to email me with all the details soon. I want to check right now."

"Let's go check."

They went out into the hallway and caught Josie's eye.

"What's the news?" Josie asked.

"My book got picked up by a publisher!" Alissa said. The words were still surreal to her.

"No way! Congrats!" Josie rushed over and gave Alissa a hug too.

"We're about to see if my professor has connected me with my editor yet if you want to come."

The three of them squeezed into Alissa's small office. Dane and Josie looked over Alissa's shoulder as she hit refresh on her email. A new one was at the top from Dr. Cane and a woman named Mandy. Alissa opened it, her heart pounding.

The email was lovely, an introduction to both Seashore Press and her editor, Mandy. Since the book was already edited, they mostly had to work on its cover, a final title, and some marketing efforts. Seeing all of the information in front of her made it all so much more real. This was finally happening. She was going to be a published author.

"This is amazing. I'm so proud of you!" Josie said. The phone rang at her desk up front. "Sorry, let me get that."

Josie slipped out of Alissa's office, leaving her and Dane alone again. Dane didn't smile a lot, so when he did, it touched Alissa's heart like nothing else. The warm, tender smile he was wearing almost brought tears to her eyes.

"I can't believe my dreams are coming true," Alissa said. "It's so much all at once. The book, the magazine, us..."

Dane sat on the edge of Alissa's desk, tucking a wild curl behind her ear. "You deserve it all."

"Thank you." She took his hand and squeezed it. The excitement spread from just her book to her entire future, especially the magazine. "I'm so excited. I think getting my book deal has inspired me in everything, especially the magazine. I want it to be great, something that people can revisit beyond the month that it was published."

"Like a coffee table magazine, almost?" Dane asked.

"Yeah, just like that! I was thinking that as much as I love having my name in print with *The Outlet*, the idea of having my name on something more long-lasting was even better. The magazine can fall somewhere in between."

"That's a great idea. Plus it's so beautiful here that we could have amazing photos and spreads that show off the beauty of the town," Dane said. "I'm sure we could find a great photographer around here."

"Yeah, maybe someone who took photos for the surf competition?" Alissa grabbed a pen and paper. "That would be perfect. And speaking of the surf competition, I was thinking of interviewing Michael and getting his story."

"Yeah? I thought about doing that for the paper ages ago, but honestly, I don't think I could get the same stories out of him that you could."

"I bet he'd be an amazing subject."

They bounced even more ideas off of each other, even coming up with rough sketches of the layout and logo of the magazine. Their ideas were ambitious —none of the other magazines in the region had done anything close to this before—but Alissa knew they had the passion and the drive to get it done. But it was going to take a while.

Eventually, Dane had to go back to his desk and get some work done on *The Outlet*, giving Alissa a chance to make some necessary phone calls. She had to let her landlord know that she was ending her lease and she wasn't coming back. And as much as she loved Literary Stays, she had to find a more permanent place to settle. Blueberry Bay was already home in her heart, but now she was going to settle in a physical home for good.

CHAPTER TWENTY-ONE

Caitlin topped off Monica and Alissa's glasses of pinot noir before attending to her own. They were gathered in the kitchen of Literary Stays, a charcuterie board, bottle of wine, and Alissa's laptop between them. Alissa had called for an impromptu gathering with wine after her publisher sent over some mock-up covers of her book.

"Here, let me show you what they sent! Seeing a cover makes it all feel so real," Alissa said, opening her computer and pulling up her email. "I think they captured the story perfectly."

Alissa opened up a file of a book cover. It had a bold, beautiful sunset with a man on the stern of a boat, looking out onto it. A siren was off in the distance, looking back at him. They hadn't settled on a final title yet, but for now, they had put in, "The Siren and the Sailor" across the top and *Alissa Lewis* at the bottom. It looked perfect and it wasn't even the final cover.

"It looks fantastic!" Caitlin said. "Their cover designer is really talented."

"She is! I got to talk to everyone on the phone on Friday and they were super nice. It's like a family." Alissa clicked over to a second mock-up, which was of the same scene at night, the moon illuminating the siren.

"I can see one of these blown up and put on an easel over in the main library," Monica said, adjusting her glasses on her nose. "And I've asked Michael over at the coffee shop about where he bought those heat lamps on the shop's patio so we could get some at a great price. Wouldn't it be great if we set up an event space so you could do a reading out here with the ocean in the background? Then we could have some themed snacks."

"That's so far off in the future," Alissa said with a laugh. "But it really would be awesome. I love being outside here, even when it's freezing."

"Plus if it's cold out, it fits the story," Monica added. Both she and Caitlin had read the draft. It was an amazing book, filled with genuine heartbreak, love, and redemption. "Like the scene where the sailor gets thrown overboard."

"I hope you're not planning on throwing any of the guests into the water," Alissa teased.

"That would be a little bit too realistic." Monica laughed, and Caitlin tried to match her energy, but couldn't. Neither her sister or Monica seemed to notice, to her relief.

While Alissa and Monica chatted about what was left in the publishing process, namely some last minute edits and marketing efforts, Caitlin sipped her wine. She was of two minds—she was excited for her sister, definitely. She was chasing her dreams and landing on her feet. Having a book published was a huge deal and the press that Alissa was working with sounded like a dream too. Alissa was finding fulfillment in what she had always wanted, which not many people got to say for themselves.

But Alissa's happiness only reminded her of how unfulfilling her life was. How she still hadn't told James when she was coming back, not that she knew herself. How she still didn't have the answers that she craved or any sense of where she wanted her life to go. The thought of finding fulfillment was so far away that it was almost laughable. As much as she loved being Pearl's mother, she wanted a piece of the life she had with James before she was born too.

Caitlin wondered if that was selfish, but didn't have an answer for that either. The questions and empty spaces in her thoughts came crashing down on her like an avalanche, making her heart pound.

"Excuse me for a second," Caitlin said, slipping away with her glass of wine.

She went outside onto the patio, the crisp air steadying her. The night was overcast, so the ocean looked like a black void that went on forever. It was soothing in a weird way despite being filled with unknowns. Steady, simple, smooth.

She sat down on the porch swing, pushing back and swinging back and forth. Her chest was tight and drinking her wine wasn't loosening the knot. Still, she tried to make that happen. She didn't want to cry out here and make Alissa think that she wasn't happy for her.

"Caitlin?" Alissa stepped out onto the porch. "You okay?"

Caitlin just shrugged and Alissa sat down next to her on the swing, rocking the chair back. The two of them sipped their wine in silence for a while as Caitlin gathered what she wanted to say.

"Are things at home still bothering you?" Alissa asked.

"Yeah. I just got overwhelmed thinking about it. It's like my entire future is hazy." Caitlin sniffed and dabbed at her eyes. "I need to go home but I'm scared to."

"That's a reasonable feeling."

"I know. But I also know that Pearl needs me and I can't avoid this forever. I have to go talk to James." Caitlin pushed off again, starting up the motion of the swing again. "It's just hard to accept that the path that I thought was going to bring me fulfillment has led me here—confused and unsure. I don't know what'll make it better or what'll bring spark back to my marriage."

Alissa took Caitlin's hand and squeezed it. Alissa's hands were warm and soft, the perfect comfort. "Maybe talking to James is just what you need to do to find answers."

Caitlin could only nod and let out a shaky breath.

"And it's normal to not know what you want or what will solve your problems. If everyone knew the answers, no one would struggle, and without those struggles no one would grow," Alissa continued. "Think about it from James's perspective too. He might be just as overwhelmed and lost as you. You both have been on this path together, side by side, and he might need to break out of his comfort zone too."

Caitlin pushed them back on the swing again. She hadn't thought about how James might be feeling–she just assumed he was fine because he acted like he was, going about his business. But what if he had been hiding it all, just like her?

"That's a good point," Caitlin said. "I've always thought of my big plans for life as stretching out of my comfort zone when in reality, they're very much within it."

They sat in silence for a few moments, the porch swing rocking them back and forth

"Josie has this quote on her desk that says, 'life begins outside of your comfort zone'." Alissa sipped her wine. "And it's true. Like with Dane, especially. Coming here was totally not a thing he would have done in normal circumstances, so that was a leap, but ever since we started working on the idea for the magazine, he's come alive. It's been great. I'm sure the same thing is waiting for you after you talk to James."

Caitlin swallowed. "I hope so. I'm going to go call James now and get ready to go home."

"Good. I'm proud of you, Caitlin." Alissa squeezed her sister's hand again.

"Thanks." Caitlin pulled Alissa into a hug. "I promise I'll be back for your book signing. And maybe I'll be a different person then."

"I know you will be. Everything will be okay."

CHAPTER TWENTY-TWO

Alissa unraveled her scarf as she walked into The Crab, looking around for Dane. The combination of meeting with him and eating delicious food had propelled her throughout her day.

Her nerves and her excitement mingled inside of her, one big ball of energy that she could hardly suppress. This meet-up was definitely a date, but Dane also told her he had some concrete ideas for the magazine that he wanted to show her. They had been throwing ideas around for a while, but Dane had taken the most potent ones and consolidated them into what he was going to show her tonight.

Alissa glanced around The Crab and spotted Dane at a table by himself in the corner, his tablet in front of him. She called his name and he looked up, his face lighting up. Dane's smile brightened Alissa from the inside out. He was even more handsome like this, his expression warm and open.

"Hey," Alissa said, leaning down and pressing a kiss to his cheek. "Have you ordered yet?"

"No, I was waiting for you. Let's go."

They put their coats down at the table Dane had chosen and went up to the front, their fingers clasped together. Hannah was at the register, and she grinned from ear to ear when she saw them together.

"Hey, guys!" Hannah said. "What can I get for you?"

Alissa looked to Dane, who gestured for her to go first. At this point, she had tried everything on the menu, and it was all equally good. Even the special sounded good, but she couldn't decide. She was so excited about getting down to work that she said, "Can you surprise me?"

"Surprise you?" Hannah's hand hovered over the register's touch screen. "With anything on the menu? Or even something on the fly?"

"Sure, why not?" Alissa looked to Dane. "I've never had anything that was less than amazing, so I know I won't be disappointed."

"Dad is going to have fun with your order."

Hannah tapped on the screen, laughing. "What about you, Dane?"

"You know what? Surprise me too," Dane said.

"All right, then." Hannah took their drink orders as well and told them the total. After some back and forth about who should pay, Dane finally passed his card over to Hannah. "I'll have your mystery orders right out to you!"

Dane and Alissa went back to their table.

"I'd say I'm shocked that you asked to be surprised too, but it feels like you've been embracing the unexpected," Alissa said, sitting down.

"I am. But also, you're right—everything here is delicious and I might as well try something new." He opened the cover on his tablet and woke it up. "Plus this plan I have is really ambitious, so I'm already taking leaps in other areas."

"I'm excited to see what you've put together." Alissa rested her forearms on the table and leaned forward. "I've been so nervous about it all day."

"Nervous?" Dane glanced up at her, one corner of his mouth quirked up. "Should I be nervous that you're nervous?""

"No, not at all! It's just a huge deal and I'm so excited, but I'm not sure of what to be excited about."

Alissa bit her bottom lip. "Is that silly? And does it make sense?"

"Sort of. I'm just glad you're excited." He tapped around on his screen and turned it so they could both do it. "I got a little bit overeager and put together a PowerPoint late last night."

"Ah, so that's why you came into the office this morning holding one hot coffee and one iced." Alissa nudged him with her knee.

"Yup. I'm not sure how I managed to pull all-nighters back in the early days of my career. Then again, it's been a little over ten years." Dane opened up his first slide. "Here we go. We threw around a lot of titles, but one really stuck with me—Coastal Views."

He showed Alissa the mockup of the logo. It was bold in its font, but the shade of blue he had chosen softened it. Alissa could easily see it on the front of a magazine.

"I love it. It looks amazing."

"Graphic design isn't really my thing, so we can get someone else to make a better one." Dane's voice held a sheepish tone to it, his neck flushing above his collar.

"It's a great start. What else do you have?" Alissa swiped to the next slide.

"This is just a mission statement I threw together."

Alissa skimmed it. It read, *Coastal Views aims to show the beauty beyond the landscape of coastal Rhode Island, highlighting the stories of the people who make this area come alive.*

It was perfect—succinct and to the point.

"I love it, Dane," Alissa said.

"I love it too." Dane's smile had an almost boyish quality to it. "Let me tell you about the editorial plan. It's a mix of your ideas and mine."

Dane launched into his next slide, which talked about the kinds of articles and the timing of each issue. Then, he moved onto the next slide, which got more technical—print runs, distribution, scaling up, and other things that made it feel like the magazine was really happening. He hardly stopped when Hannah dropped off their surprise sandwiches—a salmon burger with lemon aioli for Alissa and a twist on fish and chips in sandwich form for Dane.

The way he talked about Blueberry Bay and the area overall was so drastically different than it was when she first arrived in town. Back then, Blueberry Bay was almost a place where he had been banished. But now, he saw all of its beauty and all of the unique things and people within it. It was a place that he wanted to highlight instead of a place he just had to deal with.

Whenever Dane spoke about something he was passionate about, he got lost in it, talking with his hands, his words flowing out in a rapid stream. His grass green eyes were bright and she couldn't have taken her eyes off of him if she tried.

"Is there something wrong?" Dane asked, snapping Alissa out of her daze.

"No, nothing's wrong." She leaned across the table and pressed a soft kiss to his lips. "I just like listening to you."

Dane's cheeks flushed, but he smiled. "I'm glad I'm not boring you with this talk of profit and loss statements."

"You couldn't bore me if you tried." Alissa threaded her fingers through Dane's. "You're great at this."

"Thanks." Dane squeezed her hand. "You know, I talked to my old boss. The one that I blew up on."

"You did?"

"Yeah. He emailed me ages ago and I was too worried to open it. I wasn't as confident in my decision to be here back then," Dane said. "He basically asked me to come back and help with the paper because I had done so much to keep it going before, but I said no. This is where I belong. Here with you, doing things like this."

The warmth and affection in his voice made her tingle from the inside out. She was so elated for him —he had found himself just as much as she had, and they had found each other in the process.

"I love you," Alissa said, the words spilling out of her mouth before she could stop them.

Dane's smile grew. "I love you too, Alissa."

He leaned in and gave her another kiss. Alissa's heart fluttered and flipped in her chest, the amount of affection and excitement almost too big to fit inside of her. Not long ago, she had been sitting in her apartment with a glass of wine, pouring over job listing after job listing that wasn't quite right.

Now she was here, listening to the man she loved talk about a project that she couldn't wait to tell everyone about. She had new friends, a job that she woke up excited about every day, and tons of new experiences that she never would have gotten in Denver under her belt.

Fulfillment really came from unexpected places.

CHAPTER TWENTY-THREE

Six Months Later

The flurry of activity at Literary Stays made Dane's head spin. Monica was rushing back and forth, making sure that all the guests for Alissa's book signing had wine, beer, or their drink of choice. Hannah and Willis had catered the event, laying out trays of freshly made sandwiches on a long table outside. A gathering of volunteers set out rows of white chairs outside of the inn in intimate rows, close to the podium.

"Need help with the chairs?" Dane asked one of the volunteers.

"Sure, of course!"

Dane helped them finish up, nervous but excited energy pulsing through his veins. Alissa's book had just come out and it was already selling well. People had fallen in love with the tragic, but beautiful story of the siren and the sailor, just as Dane knew they would. The romantic storyline wasn't something he would have been drawn to, but now that he was living a love story of his own, he could appreciate it on a whole new level.

Alissa had captured the breathless excitement of falling in love perfectly, as if she had taken the way he felt for her out of his brain and put it on paper.

He glanced over his shoulder back at the bed and breakfast, the fresh summer breeze ruffling his hair. Alissa was inside with Caitlin, getting ready, and he couldn't wait to see her. Caitlin had apparently given her a makeover on their first date—which Dane had insisted wasn't a date, though in his heart he knew he wanted it to be more—so he was excited to see what Caitlin did today. Alissa was always beautiful to him either way, but seeing her dressed up was something special.

Dane wandered inside to the kitchen, where Monica was pouring more sparkling wine.

"Do you need any help?" Dane asked Monica.

"I'm good, but thank you." Monica adjusted her glasses on her nose and smiled at him. "Are you nervous?"

"What makes you say that?"

"You've been restlessly wandering around ever since you got here." Monica glanced at the drinks in front of her. "Would you like a drink?"

"Sure, I'll take some red wine." Dane chuckled to himself. "I'm just excited for Alissa."

"I am too. I know the turnout will be great." Monica passed him a glass of wine.

"And it looks great. Having it outside was the perfect choice, especially with that view in the background." Dane nodded out toward the ocean, which was going to be behind Alissa.

"Thanks!" Monica gave him a shy smile. "The moment Alissa got the book deal I was thinking of ideas for this event. I've always wanted to have something here but I never knew what event could kick it off perfectly. This is perfect."

Monica and Dane enjoyed some of their wine together before throwing themselves back into setting up. Soon, guests started to arrive, Alissa's book in hand. The more people filled the bed and breakfast's outdoor area, the more excitement buzzed in the air.

"Dane!"

Dane turned toward the person who called him over the noise of the party and to his surprise, it was Alvin. He looked happy to see him.

"Uh, hi," Dane said, unable to keep the skepticism out of his voice.

"I know, you probably weren't expecting me here." Alvin extended his hand and Dane shook it.

"How'd you hear about it?" Had news of Alissa's book spread to New York City?

"*The Outlet*. I've been following the online edition and it sounded interesting." Alvin shrugged, tucking his hands into the pockets of his khaki shorts. "I had coffee with Ross and he mentioned that you and Alissa were dating, so I figured I'd show my support."

"Wow, thank you." Dane was oddly touched.

"It's no problem at all." Alvin looked around. "I can see why you like this place. It's beautiful and calm. The way you and Alissa write about it was another reason why I came. Well that, and to talk to you. To thank you for giving me the kick I needed to get it together."

Dane blinked. He could have said the same thing to Alvin. If he hadn't been so blasé about the changes Dane wanted to make, he never would have come here. And if he hadn't come here, he wouldn't have met Alissa or found himself again.

"I'm glad I helped," was all Dane could say. To his surprise, a well of emotion bubbled up inside of him.

"Yeah. The paper's doing a lot better. I've gotten everyone under control and the standards have gone up again. And we're much more profitable as a result."

"That's amazing."

"It is." Alvin clapped him on the shoulder. "We should grab dinner soon and catch up. I'll be here for the next few days."

"I'd like that."

"I heard this place The Crab is good. Have you had it?"

Dane smiled. "It's one of my favorites."

"Perfect. How about tomorrow? I'd love to meet Alissa too in case I can't tonight."

"Sure, that sounds perfect." Dane had told Alissa some things about Alvin, especially now that they had patched things up. She would be excited to meet him.

"Good. If you'll excuse me, I think I want to grab something to drink before the event starts," Alvin said.

Dane shook his hand one more time and watched him disappear into the crowd. Something he hadn't realized was unsettled finally rested in his gut. The chapter of his life in New York City had finally come to a satisfying close without any hard feelings on either side.

Fifteen minutes before the event was going to start, Dane went upstairs to get Alissa. She had moved out of Literary Stays a few months ago, but Monica had loaned her the room where she first stayed to get ready for the event. Dane knocked on the door a few times and Caitlin poked her head out of the door. She had lost the melancholy that hovered around her six months before.

"Oh, is it time?" Caitlin asked.

"Almost." Dane peered around Caitlin. "Can I see the woman of the hour?"

"I'm right here!" Alissa popped out from behind Caitlin.

"Wow, you look incredible," Dane said once he found his voice again.

Alissa was wearing a sapphire blue sundress that was the same shade as the ocean, cinched at the waist and flaring out slightly. Her wedge sandals she was wearing popped her up to his height, though her curls added a little bit more height.

"Thank you," Alissa said, beaming.

Caitlin stepped aside so Dane could reach Alissa. He pulled her into his arms and gave her a kiss, taking care to not mess up her lipstick.

"People are arriving and it seems like they're all excited," Dane said.

"Ah, I'm buzzing out of my skin." Alissa squeezed both of his hands. "I think I should get down there."

"Let's go, then."

Dane took her hand and led her downstairs. Alissa was instantly swept away by her editor and her old professor, who had both flown in for the event. Dane let her go, watching her from across the space. Alissa had a glow about her, especially when the event officially started and she got up to read from her book.

Dane sat toward the back and discreetly took a few photos of her as she read, the wind blowing her curls around her face. After her reading, she took some questions, then the event shifted to her book signing, then finally a reception.

Dane saw almost everyone he knew in town at some point or another, chatting about the view, Alissa's book, and all of the events of the upcoming summer. Michael spotted Dane across the crowd and made his way over.

"Alissa is really talented," Michael said. "I knew it reading her articles in *The Outlet* and *Coastal Views*, but wow."

"She is." A swell of pride crested in Dane's chest.

Alissa's articles in *Coastal Views* had been a big part of its success so far. They had released two issues, both of which needed another print run to keep up with demand. People stopped him in the street all the time to talk about some articles and about what was coming up next. It had gone over better than he or Alissa had ever dreamed.

Writing about the area made him fall in love with it even more. Waking up to a quiet house, walking to work, chatting with people he saw everyday was his new normal, and he was happy with that. Add in Alissa and all of the friends he'd made, and he saw himself here for a long time.

"Speaking of..." Michael looked past Dane's shoulder. "Congratulations, Alissa."

Alissa stepped up next to Dane, her hand sliding into his.

"Thank you." Alissa smiled, raising her glass of wine. "I'm so glad you could make it."

"I wouldn't miss it." Michael looked around at the crowd. "It looks like a lot of other people feel the same way. If you'll excuse me, I want to say hello to someone before they leave."

"Thanks for coming!" Alissa said.

More people came by to congratulate Alissa and say hello—Hannah stepped away from the catering table to chat for a while, as did Monica and a few other people they knew from around town. Once they were by themselves, Dane pulled her into a hug, kissing her forehead.

"How do you feel?" Dane asked.

"I've never been so happy." Alissa rested her hand on his chest, looking into his eyes.

The warmth and happiness he felt just from looking into Alissa's eyes made him realize he hadn't been this happy before either. He woke up every day with a smile knowing he'd get to go into his office and see Alissa, create work he was proud of, and go home feeling satisfied and fulfilled.

"Same here," Dane said, kissing her again.

"You two!" Josie waved at them both, making her way across the grass. "It's so good to see you out here!"

"So good to see you too!" Josie and Alissa

hugged. "Congratulations! Hearing you reading the book makes me want to read it all over again."

"I'm so glad to hear that." Alissa let her go.

"It's crazy how you captured the energy of our town and the area. It feels like I know every last character in real life, you know?" Josie squeezed Alissa's forearm. "You really started writing it years ago?"

"Yeah, I did." Alissa shrugged. "I guess I had to be here in order for the story to come alive again."

They chatted a while longer until the event started winding down. Dane stuck by Alissa's side until the last people headed out.

"It feels so quiet here now," Alissa said from her spot on the porch.

Dane wrapped his arms around her from behind, pulling her close. "It is. It was a big event."

"So many people came."

"Because your book is great." He kissed her temple, taking in the scent of salty sea air on her skin. "Do you know what you want to do next?"

"Hmm. I want to sleep in tomorrow, for one," Alissa said with a laugh, nestling against him. "And I'm excited to see where the magazine takes us. To see how many great things we can do together."

Dane could easily see the future—their

magazine, their relationship, their lives in Blueberry Bay. It was all so filled with opportunity and hope.

"There's so much we can do." He pulled her closer, looking out onto the ocean. "I can't wait to see what we come up with."

ALSO BY FIONA BAKER

The Marigold Island Series

The Beachside Inn

Beachside Beginnings

Beachside Promises

Beachside Secrets

Beachside Memories

Beachside Weddings

Beachside Holidays

Beachside Treasures

The Sea Breeze Cove Series

The House by the Shore

A Season of Second Chances

A Secret in the Tides

The Promise of Forever

A Haven in the Cove

The Blessing of Tomorrow

A Memory of Moonlight

The Snowy Pine Ridge Series

The Christmas Lodge

Sweet Christmas Wish

Second Chance Christmas

Christmas at the Guest House

A Cozy Christmas Escape

The Christmas Reunion

The Saltwater Sunsets Series

Whale Harbor Dreams

Whale Harbor Sisters

Whale Harbor Reunions

Whale Harbor Horizons

Whale Harbor Vows

Whale Harbor Blooms

Whale Harbor Adventures

Whale Harbor Blessings

The Chasing Tides Series

(set in Blueberry Bay)

A Whisper in the Bay

A Secret in the Bay

A Journey in the Bay

A Promise in the Bay

A Moonbeam in the Bay

A Lullaby in the Bay

A Wedding in the Bay

For a full list of my books and series, visit my website at www.fionabakerauthor.com!

ABOUT THE AUTHOR

Fiona writes sweet, feel-good contemporary women's fiction and family sagas with a bit of romance.

She hopes her characters will start to feel like old friends as you follow them on their journeys of love, family, friendship, and new beginnings. Her heartwarming storylines and charming small-town beach settings are a particular favorite of readers.

When she's not writing, she loves eating good meals with friends, trying out new recipes, and finding the perfect glass of wine to pair them with. She lives on the East Coast with her husband and their two trouble-making dogs.

Follow her on her website, Facebook, or Bookbub.

Sign up to receive her newsletter, where you'll get free books, exclusive bonus content, and info on her new releases and sales!

Made in United States
Cleveland, OH
19 January 2025

13593751R00142